Alphabet Soup for Lovers

ANITA NAIR

HarperCollins *Publishers* India

First published in India in 2015 by
HarperCollins *Publishers* India

Copyright © Anita Nair 2015
Illustrations © Pinaki De

P-ISBN: 978-93-5177-482-2
E-ISBN: 978-93-5177-483-9

2 4 6 8 10 9 7 5 3 1

HarperCollins *Publishers*

A-75, Sector 57, Noida, Uttar Pradesh 201301, India
1 London Bridge Street, London SE1 9GF, United Kingdom
Hazelton Lanes, 55 Avenue Road, Suite 2900, Toronto, Ontario M5R 3L2
and 1995 Markham Road, Scarborough, Ontario M1B 5M8, Canada
25 Ryde Road, Pymble, Sydney, NSW 2073, Australia
195 Broadway, New York, NY 10007, USA

Typeset in 10.5/14.5 Electra LT Regular at
SÜRYA

Printed and bound at
Replika Press Pvt. Ltd.

For Ship & Lee
You know who you are

'It's dark because you are trying too hard. Lightly child, lightly. Learn to do everything lightly. Yes, feel lightly even though you're feeling deeply. Just lightly let things happen and lightly cope with them. So throw away your baggage and go forward. There are quicksands all about you, sucking at your feet, trying to suck you down into fear and self-pity and despair. That's why you must walk so lightly. Lightly, my darling…'

– Aldous Huxley, *Island*

Arisi – I am told that the word Arisi is what went on to become rice in English. Arisi is what we Tamizh people sustain ourselves with. It is what we seek life lessons from. Take, for instance, 'oru paana sorukku oru soru padham,' meaning, to test if a pot of rice is cooked, you need to check just one grain. Rice is what defines our week days and festive days. Sambhar rice, rasam rice, curd rice, vegetable rice, coconut rice, tamarind rice, mango rice, we have so many kinds of rice dishes and, as if that isn't enough, we turn rice into a side dish too. Of which arisi appalam is what I like best. Like vadam and vathal, arisi appalam adds a nice crunch to a meal. But unlike vadam and vathal that will last a whole year because they have been sun-dried slowly and deeply, arisi appalam tends to spoil quickly. Mould appears from nowhere and then the only thing to do is throw it into the compost heap.

Arisi Appalam

A

Arisi Appalam. I mouth the letters 'a' 'aa'. Arisi Appalam. My mouth opens like the goldfish in my granddaughter Selvi's aquarium. Ah, ah, I say it again. I think I know the 'a' well enough now. I prefer the pleasing fullness of arisi appalam to the dull crunch of the A is for Apple. A little rainbow arcs in my heart.

It's good to be back, I think, as I open the plastic bag and take out a dozen arisi appalam. I have been away for two weeks in Pollachi, where my son lives. Once I too lived in the plains but I now realize I have got used to the hills. I couldn't live anywhere else, except here in the Anamalai Hills. Arisi appalam is paper thin. Leema's eyes will light up when they are fried and on the table. Sometimes I think I can still glimpse the six-year-old girl I was brought in to look after, thirty-three years ago. I was twenty-four then. I didn't know what to call my little charge. I knew I wasn't supposed to call her by her name. She was too young for me to call her madam, so I came up with Leema, which married her name with an amma, making it sound respectful enough. I wince thinking of how Leema has been trying to teach me the English alphabet all these years. But it took Selvi, my granddaughter, to break the block in my head.

'It's no different from the Tamizh alphabet, Paati,' she said.

'Kannu, I don't know the Tamizh alphabet either,' I said, unable to keep the shame out of my eyes.

'In which case, this will be easier,' she laughed.

But I am a numbskull. My head is like a dried-up coconut…the brains have lost their ability to absorb. I realized this when I forgot yet again what F or L or T or any of the other letters of the alphabet stood for.

That's when Selvi came up with the idea. 'I know how you are going to learn the alphabet.' Her voice wobbled with excitement. 'All you have to do is match each letter with the name of a vegetable, or a fruit, or a dish. That way you'll never forget it.'

Food, I know. Food will never elude me, unlike everything else that has. Be it men, wealth, happiness and, it seems, the alphabet. I can see the possibility of what she suggests. Perhaps the alphabet can be coaxed to stay within my grasp. Perhaps food will teach me to make sense of these lines, curves and curlicues.

The arisi appalam fluffs out with a gentle fullness as I drop it into hot oil. Not smoking oil, mind you. That would leave the insides uncooked, making the appalam stick to the teeth. Arisi appalam doesn't puff up like a pappadum or a puri. Instead it turns a beautiful crisp white. It's full of flavour. Of green chillies and asafoetida, lime and the heat of the sun, and each bite is like a firecracker bursting in the mouth – salt, chilli, spice, the crunch of rice. Leema will be delighted, I know.

I peer into the dining room where Leema and her husband KK are. They are talking in hushed tones. I feel my mouth draw into a line. That's how they always are. Like two strangers in a doctor's waiting room. Not like a husband and wife who ought to rub and jostle each other like a pot within a cauldron. That's how a marriage ought to be: a bit of clang, a bit of bang, a bit of this and that, and yet when together, a perfect fit.

These two are like store-bought appalam. Seemingly perfect but with neither flavour nor taste. Leema, you need an arisi appalam in your life, I want to tell her.

1

All of that summer, it rained. And now that it's early August, the monsoon has descended on them in a whispering frenzy. It has rained all day. She doesn't mind that at all. Or that the damp has seeped into everything and that one of the rooms has sprung a leak in the ceiling. That the garden is waterlogged and the steady drip of rain from the trees has put KK in a foul mood. The truth is, she doesn't mind anything at all. That's how she has decided she will be. Lena, who has left behind the storms of her youth, all of thirty-eight years, with three grey strands on her right temple and four on the left, doesn't believe in love – the candyfloss, bonbon kind – and so is happily married.

Lena stands by the windows that flank the verandah. From the rafters beneath the eaves hang pots of begonias, geraniums and wandering jew. The monkey puzzle tree planted by the first owner, a homesick Englishman, is shrouded in mist. From within the bungalow, Lena hears faint music. KK is at his laptop. It is eleven in the morning and KK is pretending to be what he is supposed to be – a civil lawyer.

Lena turns around and looks into the house. The rain continues. She doesn't mind, except that she cannot go out for a walk. Or maybe she can, she tells herself, pulling on rubber boots and taking the raincoat down from the peg.

'I'm going for a walk,' she calls out to KK.

He looks up from his laptop. The room with its heavy wooden furniture is usually dark and sombre, but he has switched on two of the table lamps, which bathe it in their golden light. On the dining table, on the lace doily, is the centrepiece of anthurium and foxtail asparagus she had put together yesterday. KK has a mug of tea near his elbow and a frown of concentration.

'In this weather?' he asks, looking up. There is nothing querulous or whiney about the tone. It's just a matter-of-fact query: I guess you know what you are doing.

That's how the two of them are. There's an absence of messy emotions between them, the sort that can throw people off kilter. They don't question and judge and this allows them to remain wedded to each other. She looks at him and thinks: he is exactly the husband I wanted – easy on the eye and easy to be with. Am I the wife he wanted? She bins the thought in that black vault where she has shunted youthful follies and wrinkled dreams.

She shrugs. 'Doesn't look like it will stop,' she says, turning to leave.

The mist is growing thicker, but it doesn't matter. She knows her way and she has her stick with her. A stout guava stick with a pointed end and a Y at the top that gives her a firm grip. Rain falls, hushing all sound and thought. Lena walks.

Through the mist, she sees the headlamps of an SUV. A monster of a vehicle, one that doesn't belong to anyone she knows. She sees it take the fork in the road to the bungalow lower down in the valley. KK's new business venture: Ecotourism. But this is the off season and she didn't know there was a booking. Who would want to come to the middle of nowhere in the middle of the monsoon? KK had mentioned a cinema type who was looking to rent for a fortnight with the possibility of an extension if he liked the place. Nothing was decided yet, he had said. Perhaps it had come through after all.

She stands at the fork in the road, watching the vehicle inch its way down the path. It's a four-wheel drive but the driver is not used to terrain like this, she thinks with a smile. Whoever this is will have to get used to a different kind of life in the hills. Nothing prepares you for it unless you are born into it like her, or grow into it like KK.

She turns and walks towards the forest road. KK doesn't like her going towards the forest embankment on her own. 'Why take silly risks?' he says every now and then. 'It's leopard territory. At least take the dogs with you.' He doesn't ever say, don't go. But he does think he ought to caution her.

'Leopards like dog meat. It will draw them out if I take Ringo and Star with me.'

The German shepherds come running to her and nuzzle her palms, hoping she will take them with her. Ringo and Star are KK's and Lena isn't going to risk them being attacked by a leopard. Only eighteen months ago, her dog Lobo, a cocker spaniel whom she had loved more than it was possible to love anything or anybody, was taken away from the garden by a leopard one afternoon, right under her nose.

To appease KK, she always pretends she's going into the valley rather than towards the shola and so, once again, she plods up the winding road. A lone old man holding a plastic hood over his head walks towards her. He stops and waits for her to go past. 'How are you, Muthu?' she asks.

'I'm all right, Leema.' He smiles. Komathi's name for her is what everyone uses now. Muthu isn't all that old. She remembers him coming to the estate when she was a girl. He helped her mother in the garden. That was before he became the grave keeper in the English cemetery.

'Are you going up there?' he asks.

She smiles. Everyone here knows how much she likes the English cemetery.

'Do you have any tea money?' he asks, scratching the back of his neck.

She shakes her head. He doesn't need money for tea. Whatever she gives him will go towards a packet of arrack sold from the rear of the tea shop at the corner.

'Why don't you go home and ask Akka to make you a cup of tea?' she says.

'Maybe I will,' he says.

'Are you going alone towards the shola?' he asks suddenly. 'The elephants are out.'

'Oh,' she says.

'Where are you going?' she asks, trying to see through the fine rain.

Muthu shivers. 'Nowhere. You know I have nowhere to go.'

'Walk with me to the English cemetery and then you can come home with me,' she says, even though she knows KK will be annoyed. She has often wondered why KK dislikes Muthu. 'He's a harmless old man,' she tried to defend him once.

'He's a bloody drunkard!'

'Think of what he does, KK! Grave keepers drink. It's an occupational hazard. How would you feel if you had to tend to graves all day?'

But KK just walked away. They never argued because KK wouldn't allow an argument. Lena liked that best about him. He didn't lose his temper; he didn't argue. He was peaceful to be with, she had told her grandmother when she complained that KK was a cold fish.

'Vaa Muthu,' she says.

He sighs and follows her. 'Why do you like that place so much?' he asks after a few minutes.

'It's so peaceful,' she says. 'It must be nice to be buried in a place with trees, birds and blue skies above.'

He snorts and then turns it into a cough, pulling his muffler around his throat. 'When you are dead, you are dead, Leema. When you are in a hole in the ground, there are no blue skies, butterflies or flowers. It's just the wet earth and worms chewing on dead flesh.'

Lena nods. She knows this, as he does. But for a moment it was nice to envisage a heaven that felt a little like the spa resort KK and she had been to on their honeymoon fifteen years ago. A tranquillity that she felt now only in the English cemetery where the last grave was dug more than fifty years ago.

It's almost lunch time when Lena and Muthu walk back to the bungalow. The rain has stopped and a faint watery sun has emerged. At the fork in the road, Muthu peers towards the small bungalow in the valley. The road becomes a track after a few metres. The rain has turned it into a slush path. Lena hopes the guests have sturdy shoes and don't catch a cold easily. The small bungalow, now called Mimosa Cottage, was the Englishman's first home. He had built the bigger bungalow later and the small one was his Anglo-Indian overseer's quarters. KK had refurbished it, she decorated it, and their homestay experiment had begun. It's still too early to tell how it will go.

The track ends at a stream and across it is a wooden bridge that can be crossed only by foot.

For a short-stay guest, it must seem idyllic, she thinks. They won't feel the damp that refuses to dislodge from the walls of the cottage in the wet months.

'You have a guest?' Muthu asks, peering at the SUV parked beneath a tree.

'Looks like,' she says, and thinks perhaps she

can ask Muthu to pitch in as cottage servant when they have guests. But first she will need to speak to KK about it.

As Lena walks in, she sees that the table has been laid. Akka is placing the dishes on it. KK is still at the laptop, its blue light casting an ashy pallor on his face.

She glances at herself in the mirror that hangs above the sideboard. An oval face with a straight nose and wide-set eyes above a narrow forehead, framed by waist-length hair. She had her hair trimmed and set two days ago when they went down to Coimbatore.

'Do you like my hair?' she asks suddenly.

He looks at her absently. 'What? Yes, it's nice… You had something done to it?'

She makes a face. 'I had it straightened.'

'Hmm…' His eyes go back to the screen.

'Who's come to stay? You didn't tell me we were expecting a guest…' she says, surprised at the peevish note in her voice.

'Slipped my mind… Remember I said someone from the movie industry had made an enquiry. For two weeks, I was told, and with the possibility that it may extend,' KK says, snapping shut the laptop.

'So shouldn't you have gone to check if the

guest is comfortable, etcetera?' she asks, going towards the holding room, as they call it. She washes her hands at the old ceramic sink there and comes back to the dining room.

'Have you checked on the guest?' she asks again, sitting down.

KK grimaces. 'You know how I am about the movie people. Can't stand them, with their inflated egos and self-absorption. Besides, I wouldn't know what to say to them!'

Lena looks at her plate and tells herself that it isn't arrogance as much as a curious case of intense diffidence. He stands around speaking little, with an affected superciliousness that makes people recoil from him. Lena often wonders how they wound up together. Was it mostly her doing? Her need to humble the man who seemed to need little from anyone or anything?

'I was hoping that you would go across after lunch. I sent John there in the morning and he has settled the guest in,' KK says, serving himself rice and chicken curry.

Lena nods. She'll prepare a little hamper and take it across.

Her eyes fall on the plastic box that Komathi has left on the table. She opens it and sees the arisi appalam fried exactly the way she likes it, with a hint of brown at the edges. She takes one and bites into it. It crunches with a satisfying explosion of flavours in her mouth. For the first time that day, she feels a small curl of joy unfurl in her.

She looks at KK thoughtfully. He's picking at his food as if it's a minefield of hidden terrors. 'Have one of these…' she says, sliding the container towards him.

He shakes his head. 'I prefer the ones made from jackfruit.'

Why does he always want what isn't available? she thinks with a flash of irritation. And then she represses the thought with an ease that comes from long years of having shared a bed, board and roof with him. One doesn't quarrel about the smaller things in life. That's a sure way down the slippery slope, she thinks.

Badam – Probably because mundiri parpu, or cashew as Leema calls it, is more readily available, badam is seen as the superior nut. Frankly, I don't see too much of a difference. Both taste good and both turn rancid after a while. Sometimes we tend to value things and people merely because they are inaccessible.

BADAM

B

I don't think I'll ever forget a B, now that I see it as badam parpu. It's a nut I like. Not that I can afford to eat it. But each time Leema buys some, she leaves a few on a plate for me saying, 'Have it, Akka, it's good for you.'

Leema's friend brought a packet of badam from Dubai. A small bowl of it awaits me by the stove when I go to the kitchen after my afternoon nap. I smile and pick it up, then go out and sit beneath the butterfruit tree. There is a stone bench that Leema's mother built beneath it. An old bathtub sits alongside. Lilies bloom in it now. I look at the badam parpu.

They are big and plump, with fine brown sheaths, and the nuts are milky sweet. That's when I see the tall man outside the cottage. Who is he? I wonder.

There's something about him that reminds me of the badam I hold in my hand. As though he has sheathed himself and it is impossible to peel off the covering. I can't see his face though. He is too far away.

I see him stride towards the cliff's edge and my heart goes into my mouth. What is he thinking? I stand up.

Should I call out to caution him? Voices carry easily in the hills.

Then I see him turn and walk back towards the house.

2

He walks into the cottage and looks at himself in the mirror. For the first time in many weeks, he feels an overwhelming sense of relief. The man in the mirror isn't the man everyone knows. He touches his shaven head with almost a sense of wonder. Why hasn't he ever done this before?

The homestay people seem non-intrusive. He had feared they would want to make friends, take photographs, have him sign autographs and once again it would begin – that whirl of adulation that comes with stardom. But only an Assamese man, who said his name was John, had come to give him the keys and show him around. 'The switch for the hot water is here. And this is the kettle if you would like to make tea. Breakfast, lunch and dinner will be served here. Do let us know if you have any preferences,' he had said, even as Shoola Pani hurried him towards the door.

He pulls a chair closer to the window and sits down. The man had turned on a table lamp. A small pool of yellow lights up a corner of the room. Otherwise the room is in darkness even though it's almost noon.

Shoola Pani shuts his eyes and thinks of the cameras and lights, the countless people, the pointless chit-chat with hangers-on and guests, the retreat into his caravan; even there they came – the producers and directors, screenplay writers and guests from overseas, proffering invitations, awards. And each one of them wanting some of the tinsel shimmer they saw him bathed in. Eventually he was unable to deal with it.

At first he began to have difficulty sleeping. And then an increasing feeling of fatigue. He lost his temper with the assistant directors and snarled at the director. His make-up assistant and PA seemed like prison guards. He eyed his teenage children with hostility and wondered why they were so needy despite being provided with everything. His wife, who lived on another continent – running a dance school – had it easy, he thought with a bitterness he had never felt before. For three weeks a year, they played husband and wife while they went on holiday: a river cruise on the Danube, a safari holiday in Kenya… They drank innumerable cocktails, made desultory conversation, shopped and made love a few times and for the rest of the year he was left to deal with life on his own.

And then the freeze happened during the last

shot of his call sheet for the film. It was a simple enough scene. He was to stand staring at the horizon. A series of emotions would play out on his face as he thought of all that had brought him there. Only, when 'Action' was called, he felt his face go taut and turn numb as if someone had poured plaster of Paris on it. As a movie star, he was known for emoting with a flick of an eyebrow. They called him a real actor because he breathed a character through every fibre of his being. Only, that morning the real actor had turned wooden as a mannequin at a store window. His muscles refused to move and his mind refused to feel; only the words came – syllables of gibberish, he thought.

There was a moment of silence. Was it disbelief or incredulity? He didn't know. The truth was, he didn't care. All he felt was a great weariness and an overwhelming desire to flee. If he could get away, he thought, he would try and make sense of what was happening to him. He was on edge as they packed up for the day. He felt he would explode if he had to utter one more nicety to one more person. The financier of his next film was waiting in his caravan, an oily smile on his fat face. It was the smile of a man who had just taken possession of a valuable artefact. That was how Shoola Pani felt.

Like a commodity. He had ceased to be a man. He was a star, and his star value was what everyone wished to grab for themselves. As he stood there with the oily financier, smiling and posing for a photograph, he suddenly thought of a place a director friend of his had mentioned.

'Amazing location. Just tea estates and shola. The place doesn't have a movie theatre within a forty-kilometre radius. No movie posters or hoardings. The workers are mostly from Assam or Jharkhand and they know nothing about south Indian cinema. So even someone like Runa,' he said, mentioning his current squeeze, a Miss India who had become the wonder girl of Tamizh cinema, 'goes unnoticed. In fact, I think after the initial euphoria of being left alone, she was quite annoyed about being ignored!'

The director sipped his beer and described the location. 'There's a homestay there. I am quite tempted to go away and rent the place for a couple of weeks to work on my new script.'

Shoola Pani had barely paid attention then. But suddenly it seemed like the one place in the world he most wanted to be. The director had given him a number. He told Tony, his make-up man, and Biju, his PA, to book the cottage for two weeks. It was for a friend of his, he said.

Shoola Pani woke up a little past two in the morning. The sleeping pill hadn't worked that night either. He picked up his mobile. 'Can you come?' he said as if it were two in the afternoon.

'I'll be there in twenty minutes,' Tony said. Being a superstar's make-up man had its joys and sorrows. His boss wasn't as much of an arsehole as some others were reputed to be. Nevertheless, he was a child when it came to having his whims pandered to.

'I want you to shave my head as well as my moustache,' Shoola Pani said when Tony arrived, ignoring the horror in Tony's eyes.

'But…' Tony began.

Shoola Pani walked towards the bathroom, not bothering to respond. Tony followed, unable to understand what was being asked of him.

Shoola Pani sat on a bath stool. Tony wondered if he had cutting shears in his kit. He was a make-up artist, not a bloody barber. He rummaged through and found one still in its blister pack. Why had he even bought it?

Tony began cutting bits of the actor's hair off. The floor began to come alive with hair trimmings. Shoola Pani felt a curious sense of flatness as he watched his hair fall around him. Once, the sight of a stray hair on his pillow would have petrified him.

Tony wrapped a towel around Shoola Pani's shoulders. A grey-black strand caught on the towel. For years Shoola Pani had nurtured his hair like an exotic pet. He had fed it and groomed it with a sense of fear pawing at his throat: Would it fall? Would his hairline recede? Would he need to wear a toupee or a wig like most other superstars?

Tony pulled out the electric trimmer and its whirrring sound filled the bathroom. 'Are you sure?' he asked, hesitating once again.

Yes, I have never been surer, he thought. 'Get on with it,' he growled.

He packed a small suitcase and, on a whim, dropped his iPad in. He needed a book, he thought, and that's when it hit him: he didn't own any. Actually, he couldn't remember when he had read a book last.

He drove himself. At the petrol pump he stopped to fill the tank up. He watched, amazed, as the Land Cruiser guzzled up petrol. Why did he need a vehicle like this? he asked himself. There was a moment of disquiet when the boy at the pump peered at him, then looked away. Shoola Pani exhaled.

Late in the afternoon, he stepped out to look around. Behind the cottage a hill rose steeply. A little past his front door was a precipice. He could see acres and acres of tea bushes and all around was the stillness of a day wreathed in rain and mist. He walked to the cliff's edge. What if he stepped over? Who would care?

Shoola Pani stands up, stricken by a strange restlessness. The silence of the cottage booms in his ears. The phones in his home and Biju's mobile wouldn't have stopped ringing, he thinks with a grim smile of satisfaction. His PA has been instructed to say that he has gone to Europe. He doesn't want the media speculating.

'I don't want to be disturbed,' he told Biju firmly.

'When will you return?' Biju asked, unable to hide his dismay.

'When I am ready,' Shoola Pani mumbled.

Will he ever be ready to return to that life, he wonders as he turns the light switch on and off, on and off, till the bulb blows a fuse.

He wonders if there is a spare bulb somewhere in the cottage. If he finds one, will he remember how to change a light bulb?

How had he let himself become this empty shell of a man?

Cheppankizhangu – Leema calls it colocasia. She said it has been cultivated in our land for more than ten thousand years. I would have thought that after many thousand years there would be a whole granary of recipes for cheppankizhangu, instead of which we have just enough to count on the fingers of one's hand. I wonder if it's because it is buried under the soil. Out of sight. Out of mind. Who knows?

CHEPPANKIZHANGU

C

I rummage through the basket of cheppankizhangu. I could make a morkozhambu with it, or roast it. A cat mews at the door. It's a stray I feed every now and then. C for cat, my alphabet book says, but I think my C will be cheppankizhangu.

The cheppankizhangu grows beneath the soil, several babies attached to a mother tuber. That's what they called me. A little knob of a cheppankizhangu clinging to its aachi. When I was six years old, my aachi showed me how to pick the perfect cheppankizhangu. Look for the plump, rounded ones, not the hairy, knobbly ones; they will be mealy in the mouth. I was too young to understand then but aachi was giving me a life lesson in the guise of a cooking lesson.

People are the same. The hairy, knobbly ones

and the plump, rounded ones. Not their bodies but their souls. Take Leema. She pretends to be a hairy, knobbly person when what she is, is plump and rounded. There is a huge reservoir of feelings within her, which she keeps hidden behind that stiff exterior.

Do you know how we clean the cheppankizhangu? We put it in a cloth and beat it against a stone. The skin flakes off then. Someday I hope that this woman, whom I brought up, will emerge from where she has hidden herself. But first, someone will need to flake the skin off. With patience and some violence.

Like my aachi would say, you can't make an omelette without breaking eggs.

3

Komathi had left the containers on the table. A small slab of badam-halwa, some chips and her famous cheppankizhanguvaruval, which one could eat as an accompaniment to curd rice or snack on with a cup of tea. Lena smiles at Komathi's choice. She hopes their guest won't turn down his nose at it. Not everyone likes these old-fashioned treats.

The rains had stopped over the night and a thin mist hangs in the air. KK has gone to the Anamalai Club. Lena pulls on a thin fleece over her T-shirt and laces her sneakers.

'Why do you dress so shabbily?' Komathi says from the corridor. 'All those nice clothes and saris hanging in the almirah and you still wear these faded baggy things! At least put some powder on your cheeks!'

Lena frowns. Komathi's notion of powdering her cheeks is slathering talc on as if she were a Kabuki dancer. 'Why? I'm just going to drop this off and head out for my walk.'

When she sees that Komathi won't budge, as if to assuage the older woman, she pulls out a tube of Vaseline and smears it on her lips.

Komathi shakes her head. 'There is no changing you!'

'I don't want to change, Akka,' Lena says softly. The firmness in her voice makes the older woman flinch.

The dogs bound ahead. It's time she introduced them to the guest. At the little bridge, they wait for her. 'C'mon,' she says as she crosses the bridge. The curtains are drawn at the cottage and there's no sign of anyone inside. Through a narrow gap in the curtains Lena sees a man sitting by a window overlooking the valley. A table lamp is on but the rest of the room is shrouded in darkness.

She knocks. A few minutes later, the door opens. She stares at him in disbelief. 'Oh my god…' she says, wondering what one of the best-known movie stars in the country is doing in her cottage. He has shaved his head and removed his trademark moustache, but there is no mistaking him.

He doesn't speak. She takes a deep breath and begins again, 'Hello, I am Lena Abraham. I dropped in to welcome you to Mimosa Cottage.'

He nods. 'Would you like to come in?'

As she follows him in, he says in a voice laced with resentment, 'I suppose there's no getting away from who I am.'

'I suppose you want an autograph,' he continues with what looks suspiciously like a sneer.

'Why would I want one?' she says in a soothing voice, as if she were talking to a growling dog.

'Everyone I meet seems to want one. And then they want me to pose for a photograph with them which they will then post on Facebook or tweet with the caption: with my good friend, superstar Shoola Pani Dev.'

Lena stares at him. Then she asks, careful to hide her annoyance, 'Are you always this rude?'

He glares at her. No one has spoken to him like this for god knows how long. The deference in most people's voices and eyes grates on his nerves. It makes him ruder, wanting to see how much further he can push them. Suddenly he feels a queer sense of ease; the freedom he had sought may be his after all.

'I apologize.' He grins. 'I think I've forgotten how to be anything but rude.'

Lena sees a glimmer of boyishness in his face.

He takes a deep breath and stretches his hand out to her. 'Hello, I am Shoola Pani Dev, the runaway actor.'

Her mouth quivers with amusement. She places her hand in his. 'Hello, Shoola Pani Dev, runaway actor, I am Lena Abraham.'

'And?'

'And nothing…' she says firmly.

'That's it?' He cocks his head. 'No descriptor?'

'No descriptor,' she says cryptically and places the basket she has brought on a low table. 'With compliments from the house,' she says.

'This is a beautiful place,' he says, dragging another chair towards the window and gesturing for her to sit.

'Yes, there's a serenity here that you won't find in many places,' she says.

A silence creeps between them. Lena thinks she must puncture it. She points to a stately old fig tree growing by the edge of the cliff and says, 'I love that tree.'

'I love that tree.'

She is startled. He has spoken the very same words.

They look at each other. It's as if the two of them have just felt a delicate contouring of their souls.

Daangar Chutney – When you first eat Daangar chutney, you wonder what the fuss is all about. It's just a pachadi or raita, as KK would call it. The Marathi people who went to live in Thanjavur can't seem to do without it. So I suppose it must be an acquired taste, like coconut oil.

DAANGAR CHUTNEY

D

Leema comes home with an expression that puzzles me. I glance at the kitchen clock. I can read time. Almost. She has been away for two hours. Usually she comes back from her walk in an hour's time.

'Where were you?' I ask.

'Nowhere,' she says, not quite meeting my eye.

'How can you be nowhere? You were away somewhere for the last two hours.'

'Akka, it's been so long since you made Daangar chutney. Will you?'

There's a gleam in her eye and the corners of her mouth bloom. When she was a child, she often dipped into the honey jar with a large spoon when no one was looking. I would see her emerge from the storeroom and there it would be – that same expression of stolen pleasure. My Leema is too old to find joy in the sticky sweetness of honey. What has she been stealing?

'I would,' I say. 'But I've forgotten how to.'

'I think Mummy has it written down. Let me look for it,' she says, almost skipping to the door. My eyebrows rise.

I had forgotten about daangar chutney. All day, I had thought that when it came to the alphabet D, I would have to settle for dosa, but a D reminded me of a folded dosa and that didn't feel right. But here it is now, D on a plate. Or should it be a bowl, I chuckle to myself.

I don't particularly like daangar chutney.

It reminds me too much of Raghavendra Rao, the man who taught me how to make it. It isn't really one of our dishes, it's a Marathi one. And he was a Maratha. 'In Thanjavur, there's a large number of us, and we still eat like our forefathers did.'

'And how is that? With your elbows?' I had asked saucily. I didn't know myself around him. He made me feel like I was eighteen with my whole life stretching ahead of me.

'Don't be cheeky,' he said, tugging at my plait.

I knew where this was headed. The joking and unnecessary touching, the knowing glances and secret smiles. I knew there would be nothing but heartbreak. But I still walked into it with my eyes wide open. And now I can't even remember the one thing he left me with. Daangar chutney.

4

Neither of them can understand it.

Not Lena, who has often scoffed at the notion of sitting across from a man and thinking that you don't ever want to let him, or that moment, go. Of suddenly wanting to reach across and run her finger along the length of his nose. Of smelling his cologne and wanting to drink deep of the fragrance of his skin.

Nor Shoola Pani, who has acted the scene countless times in front of the camera, all the while thinking that the actress really needs to do something about her acne scars. Or that the real-estate man hasn't called him with the final price for the plot of land he is looking to buy on the ECR waterfront in Chennai. For the first time, though, he looks at the woman sitting across from him and wants her to meet his gaze as if she means it. He wants to take her soft, full lower lip between his fingers and fold it into an accordion pleat.

Neither of them can understand the density of the moment until they both rise abruptly from their chairs and he asks with what she thinks is awkwardness hinging on the offensive, 'Can I trust you?'

'What?' Lena's eyes widen.

'You won't tell anyone I am here,' he says, going back to being the movie star, paranoid, persecuted and surly.

She laughs with incredulity at his behaviour and walks out of the door. Bastard, the supercilious bastard, she thinks.

He watches her leave with a queer pang. What has he done? 'Please,' he calls out. 'I apologize.'

'Will you come back? I was going to make some coffee…' he improvises, remembering the jar of instant coffee.

She pauses, and not knowing why, turns to walk back towards him. He smiles.

She drinks his coffee even though it tastes bitter and artificial. And they talk till she glances at the clock and sees it's late. Halfway through the door, she turns and says, 'You can trust me, you know. Why would I want to share you with the rest of the world?'

She flees then, unable to believe what she has just said. That wasn't what she meant to tell him, but the words had tripped off her tongue, heedless of what they sounded like or what he would think. And yet, she didn't regret one syllable.

*

He says her name: Lena. That's what the whole world calls her. He must have a name for her that's his. Lee: he says it to gauge how it sounds. It feels like a promise on his tongue. A strange sense of elation runs through him. All through these two hours, it felt like the wall he had built around himself was cleaving and crumbling. A certainty that there is something to life after all: sensations, feelings, and the possibility of emotions that aren't merely make-believe.

In her home, in the quiet of her bedroom, Lena gazes at herself in the old-fashioned full-length mirror fitted into the bureau. Her cheeks are flushed. Why? she asks herself sternly. Because she has made an ass of herself in front of one of India's best-known movie stars. What was she thinking? She groans and sinks onto the bed, holding her head in her hands. Then she looks at herself in the mirror again and sees the sparkle in her eyes. She leaps up and goes to the kitchen.

Komathi is standing by the kitchen door, staring at the avocado tree. She has a faraway look in her eyes. 'Akka,' Lena asks, 'shall we start on the daangar chutney?'

Komathi sighs and returns from that faraway place where she was with her Rayar. That was her name for him.

'What is this craving for daangar chutney? I don't remember it being a favourite of yours.' Komathi frowns, watching Lena look through a recipe book.

She shrugs. 'I don't know, I just felt like eating it…' she says, turning away so Komathi can't see her flushed cheeks.

Shoola Pani mentioned how much he liked daangar chutney and that he hadn't eaten it since his mother died years ago. No one knows how to make those old-fashioned dishes any more, he said softly. She heard the undertone of regret and thought that he didn't much like his life. He was like a wild animal, a leopard trapped in a circus, unable to leave, unable to belong. She had felt a great yearning to gather him in her arms. Instead, she decided to surprise him with daangar chutney.

'He doesn't like it,' Komathi says, as she measures out the urad dal for the flour.

'Who?'

'Who? Himself…your husband,' Komathi sniffs.

'Oh.' Lena waves her hand airily. 'Make him some of that date chutney he likes!'

'When you try to please everyone, you end up pleasing no one,' Komathi says under her breath.

Lena smiles. 'I am pleasing just myself here. Besides, it's only a chutney.'

But is it just a chutney? she will ask herself later.

Eeral – For us Tamizh people, eeral is prized meat. When I was a young wife, I ate it a lot. Mutton liver pepper fry, mutton liver masala...my mouth waters at the very thought of it. But we don't eat it very much here, in this house. Perhaps that explains why KK and Leema are the way they are.

EERAL

E

Leema's grandmother, whom I call Ammachi, once told me that in Kerala, where she is from, they don't see the heart as the place where love comes to rest. 'What is a heart, Komathi? Just a pump. The liver decides who we are.

'Blood flows into the liver and away from it, taking with it all that our body needs and making us who we are: melancholic or phlegmatic, choleric or sanguine. Without the liver we are nothing but a mass of flesh. So it is with our liver we love.'

I didn't understand what she meant. Perhaps I wasn't meant to understand and she was merely speaking her thoughts aloud. Perhaps all she wanted of me was that one day I would repeat it to her granddaughter. That an organ the size of one's fist shouldn't be allowed to dictate the course of one's life. Instead, look elsewhere, towards the liver perhaps. It is the heaviest organ in the body apart from the skin. If it functions, so do you. Or you turn wan and yellow and die. Even I know that. And so I think Ammachi may have been right after all. With the heart, you invest in another person. With your liver, you invest in yourself, and if you don't love yourself, how can you love someone else?

Leema must have a baby soon, I decide. She has already left it too late, but perhaps that will right her world. I know that KK is the reason why there isn't a child. He is opposed to the idea of adoption. I think she needs more liver in her diet. That's what the ancients have taught us. If your leg aches, have mutton soup. If you have to build your constitution, eat mutton liver. When you build your constitution, you build your gumption. That is the truth. Then it strikes me that I have an ingredient for the letter E. Eeral, for that's what we call liver in Tamizh.

I have always relished eeral varuval. It is an easy dish to cook, but you can just as easily ruin it. The liver is a strange organ that can be tender or tough, and it needs to be treated with care, for there is only so much it can take. So you don't salt the offal as you broil it and you don't cook it too long.

Leema, I would tell her, you must learn to treat

yourself with the consideration you shower on everyone else. Treat yourself with kindness, child. But she won't heed my words. I am too familiar for her to perceive any real value in what I have to say. And then I know what I must do. I am going to ask Muthu to bring some liver from near the dam, where they have a mutton stall once a week, and I will tell Leema what goes into the cooking of liver.

I will show her what happens when you let it simmer on a slow fire without stirring it. What neglect can do to the liver and soul. No one likes a tough piece of meat, not even my Leema.

Falling in love with a man is easy; what isn't is to love yourself. Girl, love yourself or you will end up like me. With a tough piece of meat as a heart and worn-out shoe leather for a soul.

5

Lena thinks she has been imagining it all as she walks towards his house. For some reason, she can't think of him by name. She sees his face swimming in her mind. 'Stop it,' she says aloud, tossing her hair from her face. 'You are thirty-eight years old, not a silly teenager to be mooning over a movie star.'

When her best friend in school made scrapbooks filled with newspaper clippings, photographs and trivia about her favourite movie stars, she had laughed at the blind hero worship and wide-eyed adulation. He isn't for real, she admonished her. You would be better off responding to the overtures of the boy from the coffee shop. Her best friend went on to marry the boy from the coffee shop. And she, here she is walking across the bridge to the door of a man whose photographs fill the scrapbooks of innumerable girls.

He opens the door even as she steps onto the gravel path leading to the cottage. She blinks. Has he been waiting for her? He smiles. 'Hello.'

'I thought you would come by yesterday, in the evening,' he says.

I had to hold myself back, she wants to tell him. Give this, whatever seems to have sprung up between us, some semblance of sanity. Instead she says carefully, 'I suppose you are not used to being on your own.'

She sees how the stubble covering his scalp is a mélange of black and white. It makes his face seem younger than ever. She has an irresistible urge to stroke his face and run the back of her palm over his head.

He doesn't respond to her comment, but cocks his head and says, 'You look nice.'

She blushes. She had washed her long hair the evening before but the straight as rainwater hair had gone back to being a mass of curls. This morning, she had pulled on a chiffon tunic in a deep aubergine instead of her habitual T-shirt and hooked two silver hoops in her ears. I am dressing for him, she told herself with a little flutter in her chest. What am I doing? I am a wife. I have a life.

'You should have come over,' she says.

'I did think of it.' His face reveals nothing. He is an actor, she tells herself. Pretense is his art form. Perhaps I can trust him when his face says nothing.

'Do you want to go for a walk with me? No one will know you,' she says, seeing the hesitation in his eyes. 'Most of our workers are from Jharkhand or Assam.'

He nods. 'I know. That's why I chose to come here.'

They walk in silence for a while. Once again she sees in him the caged wild animal set free. His gait is that of a leopard, she thinks. A sure-footed stealthiness. He is afraid and wary, she realizes. Just as a leopard weaves its way through the light and shade in the shola, he too seeks to be invisible, wanting to merge with the shadows and not be seen.

'This way,' she says, coaxing him away from the road that leads to the town.

She sees him raise his face to the skies. A pale sun has emerged through the clouds. She pulls out a floppy hat folded into four from the back pocket of her jeans.

There is a teasing glint in his eyes. 'I did wonder why one side of your butt was swollen.'

She flushes. 'Do you want it?' she asks, pretending nonchalance.

He frowns. 'Why?'

'Don't movie stars have to protect their looks?'

He makes a face that has her spluttering with laughter. 'Sorry,' she says in a tone she doesn't recognize. Who is this girl-woman?

He takes the floppy hat from her hands and places it firmly on her head. 'Walk,' he says.

She strides ahead of him. Will he pant as they trudge uphill? 'It's a stiff climb,' she says, turning towards him.

'I can see that.'

'There is another path. But it isn't as pretty,' she says, wondering if she should have taken him towards the valley rather than the shola. 'And we may spot animals on this route.'

'Monkeys?'

'Bison. Sometimes even elephants or a leopard,' she says softly. 'So don't wander this way on your own. It isn't safe.'

He smiles at her. 'And you think I'm safe when I'm with you?'

She gasps.

'What?' he asks with an innocent expression.

'Nothing.' The corners of her mouth lift in a secret smile.

'Madam, are we going to stand here and talk or are we going to walk?' He takes her hand in his and leads the way.

What is happening? she asks herself, feeling the warmth of his fingers as they clasp hers. He is a movie star; such casual caresses mean nothing to him. He enacts love and hate in front of total strangers; weeps tears for parents and children who are not his; swears eternal friendship with people he wouldn't deign to pass the time of the day with… Do not read more into this, Lena, she tells herself, crumpling her exhilaration into a ball of impassivity, and sliding her fingers out of his.

Filter Kaapi – There are just a few things that we Tamizh people need on a daily basis. If we need rasam to complete our meal, we need filter coffee to sparkle up our day. When I came to this household first, they all drank tea or instant coffee. But once they drank my filter coffee, it was all they wanted. KK came back from one of his trips to Pollachi, saying, 'I prefer your coffee to what I had at Amudha Surabhi. What is the secret, Akka?' I smiled. I wasn't going to tell him that I added a pinch of jaggery to the sugar. Instead I smiled and said, 'Kaipunyam…what else?'

FILTER
KAAPI

F

I step into the kitchen and am greeted by the aroma of freshly brewed kaapi.

I stare at the steel filter that is out on the kitchen table. Where did that come from? We haven't used it in a long time.

When I was put on homeopathic medicines a few months ago for my gout, the doctor said I should stop drinking filter kaapi. I had no intention of listening to him, but to appease him I said I would. But the next morning when I came into the kitchen, I found the filter had been stashed away.

Leema looked at me, trying to hide her smile and said, 'Since you are not supposed to drink coffee, I decided it was too much of an effort for you to make it just for the two of us. You can make us instant coffee!'

I knew she knew that I hated the taste of instant coffee. You might as well drink dish water, I would say. I realized then she was making sure that I didn't drink coffee.

I inhale deeply and think of the letter F. How it stands tall and proud. My F would be Filter Kaapi. Brewed with coffee powder that was 80 per cent arabica and 20 per cent chicory. I imagine this must be how heaven smells.

I look at Leema. But she is lost in thought. 'Leema,' I say.

She looks at me, not really seeing me.

'What happened?'

'I have a guest coming in later in the morning. I don't think he likes instant coffee.' She doesn't meet my eye.

'Who is this guest?' I ask, wondering at the radiance on her face and where she had managed to source the coffee powder from.

'The guest at the cottage. I asked him over for coffee,' she says.

'The actor?' I ask.

'You know he is an actor?'

'I recognized him. My granddaughter has a picture of him on her cupboard!'

She begins to rinse out the coffee pot. It is only

seven in the morning. Why is she setting out the tray with the coffee pot and mugs? Then I remember how I used to scour the steel glass and davara so it shone like silver and keep it ready for Raghavendra Rao to serve him his coffee as soon as he came looking for me.

We women are so naïve, I think. We forget who we are when we let a man find a place within us.

I am curious about the actor. It has been only three days since he came to stay, but he seems to have cast a spell over my Leema. I suppose he has nothing else to do but charm her and it is natural for Leema to have her head turned by a famous actor paying her such undivided attention. And KK, does he see the transformation in her? He is a strange creature, that man; seeing only what he thinks he ought to see. But even he can't be oblivious to the stars in her eyes. Or does he think filter kaapi put it there?

6

He feels as if he is stepping in front of the camera for the first time. How do you speak? What do you say? Will she hear what he thinks? Will she sense what he feels? He is wearing a pair of camel-coloured corduroy trousers and a pale yellow half-sleeved shirt. Does it make him look wan and sallow? The shadows beneath his eyes have begun to fade but there is still a bleakness within that he is unable to shrug off.

Then he sees her. She is standing framed by a window around which a creeper grows. Green leaves and a thick vine that swirls and curls. He sees her hair that he so wants to run his fingers through. It swirls and curls like the creeper. He sees her fingers tap a secret song. He wonders what the nape of her neck would feel like. But most of all, he sees the seriousness in her eyes as she stares into the distance.

He thinks of what she said to him the evening before. He had asked her who she would want to be if she had another chance to re-live her life and she had said softly, "'I don't want to be good; and I don't want to be bad: I just don't want to be bothered about either good or bad: I want to be an active verb.'"

He had felt his eyebrows rise. 'Wow!'

'Oh no, these are not my words. Bernard Shaw's, in fact! It's all I remember from my college days!' She had laughed.

She raises her head and sees him. A smile begins in her eyes. He sees her transform into an active verb. He feels it too. Something flips within him. All these years of acting out this scene, the man falling in love, haven't prepared him for this. A jet engine of headiness seems to hurl through him as he takes the last few steps to her door in a rush, propelled by its sheer intensity and power. And she, she opens the door just as his foot is on the first of the three steps that lead towards her door.

She smiles. He smiles. In the distance, thunder rumbles. In a grammar book somewhere, two active verbs collide.

He follows her into the house, his gaze taking in little details – the wooden sofas and the low coffee table, the rocking chair and the old-fashioned turning bookcase. The walls are a faded ivory. The heavy drapes have been pulled aside to let the sun into the room through a window that opens to another view of the valley. Net curtains that start halfway down the window frame puff gently with the breeze. The room is shabby but charming in an old-fashioned way. He thinks of his mansion by the sea and all that it contains. So much of everything and such little soul. He goes towards the window. He doesn't like these thoughts that have begun to trouble him.

She joins him there.

'You can see my cottage from here,' he says in surprise.

'Umm…' she says. 'It used to be the overseer's cottage and the Englishman liked to keep an eye on him.'

He glances down at her. She is biting her lip. 'Don't,' he wants to say, resisting the urge to stroke that lip. Instead he goes to sit on one of the sofas.

'Coffee,' she says brightly.

She goes away and he sits there wondering if this is for real, or a movie set. Then the aroma of filter coffee rushes up his nostrils and he sees her at the end of the trail. Bearing on a tray a tall coffee pot covered with a cosy, two chunky mugs and a plate of biscuits.

He rises to help her. He remembers he did something like this in a movie once. Is life mirroring the movies or is it vice versa?

'It's all right. I can manage,' she says, briskly side-stepping him and placing the tray on the table.

She pours the coffee and offers one mug to him. He takes it and cups it in his palms. From the garden someone whistles. His eyes dart towards the sound. She smiles at him. 'The Malabar whistling thrush.'

He raises an eyebrow. 'I've been wondering for the last two days about the boy who seems to be whistling all the time.'

She grins widely. 'That's what they call the bird. The whistling schoolboy.'

He takes a sip of the coffee. Is coffee an aphrodisiac, he wonders as something stirs in him. He exhales slowly to rein in his impulse to lean forward and kiss her. 'It's delicious,' he says. 'Hmm…not just beauty and brains.' He pauses. 'She can also make the world's best filter kaapi!'

She kicks off her sandals and curls up on the sofa, nestling the coffee mug between her palms.

'Is there anything you don't know?' he asks. He means it as a joke.

But she is serious when she says, 'Plenty. I know a lot of useless trivia, but of what really matters, I don't know much.'

He wonders what has scarred her so. There is a fragility to her that makes him want to gather her into his lap and cuddle her as if she were a child.

His glance meets hers.

Komathi, who is hovering by the door to take a closer look at the actor, feels the insides of her mouth go dry.

Godumai – At first, when I came to work here, I was horrified at what I found in the kitchen. Big bins of atta and a small bin of rice. Was I expected to stop eating rice? How could I? I ate rice three times a day. Freshly cooked rice for lunch, the leftovers for dinner, and what was left of that, I would pour water into and keep it for the morning. I would add some buttermilk, a slit green chilli, and have it for breakfast. It was the start I needed to put in a good day's work. The godumai atta as well as the small bin of basumati rice was for the family. And here is your rice, Leema's mother had said, showing me a bin of ration-shop rice. It was exactly what I was used to. I sighed in relief.

GODUMAi DOSAi

G

Early in the evening, I come to the kitchen, wondering about dinner. I don't need to cook. Leema and KK have gone out to meet someone on another estate. What I want is comfort food; something that will reassure me that the epicentre of my world hasn't shifted.

I hate change. I always have. But God in his heaven, in his white veshti with its zari border, twirling his handlebar moustache when not tugging at his chest hair, peers down at me and says in a voice that is as malicious as it is amused, 'Komathi, since you dislike change, sending you some... Enjoy, Kannu, enjoy!

For years Leema and her mister, her KK, have lived this life in their neatly patterned boxes. I have often wished something would happen to bring her alive, inject some energy into their Dettol life. For that is how I see their lives – sterile, clean and dull. But God, who seems to me more and more like a bored pannaiyar, is up to some mischief. Leema and that actor... What is going on? And doesn't KK see any of it? Or is he seeking a way to escape their life too? I feel bile crawl up my throat. What will I do if their lives fall apart? Where will I go?

I think of my aachi. The day I was turned down by the first man who came to view me as a prospective wife, she looked at my crestfallen face and said, 'Avankadakaran!'

'What?' I asked, surprised by her belligerent tone. I had thought she would blame me for the rejection. I felt as though I had failed her.

'Let him be...' she said. 'Did you see him? Like a kathrikai that has grown arms and legs – short, squat and swarthy!"

I smiled at the idea of a brinjal with arms and legs. He did look like that.

'And instead of falling at my feet and pleading with me to be allowed to marry you, he has the nerve to reject you. He doesn't deserve you,' she said.

'What do I deserve?' I asked, unable to hide my misery.

'This,' she said, beginning to mix a batter of godumai-maavu, salt and water. She added a handful of powdered jaggery and a lone cardamom. The memory of those godumai dosai, crisp yet chewy, sweet and salty, that burnt sweet smell of jaggery turning to syrup on a hot cast-iron tava… My mouth waters.

Both KK and Leema use the tava to make their eggs – bullseye and flipped over. I have told them they mustn't and that the dosa tava should be treated like an aged grandparent, oiled and brought out only for specific reasons, but neither of them heeds my words. So my godumai dosai clings to the griddle even though I try and tease it out with large dollops of oil. It leaves a little of itself behind. Like a G, I think with a giggle. Torn in the middle, with the torn bit hanging on the side.

As I eat my godumai dosai, I think I can handle whatever my pannaiyar god is lining up for me.

7

Shoola Pani has an email. It's from his PA, who
thinks he must keep him informed. Biju would find
him even if he were to hide under a rock in the
seventh chamber of hell, Shoola Pani thinks with a
flash of irritation. The advertising agency is getting
restless for a date for the TV commercial shoot. He
is the brand ambassador for a high-end watch and
they have paid him a lot of money. They are making
close to threatening noises, Biju wrote.

Shoola Pani picks up his phone with his unlisted
number. 'Biju,' he says into the phone, 'tell them I
have leprosy.'

He hears the horror in Biju's voice as he splutters,
'I can't tell them that, sir.'

'Tell them I have jaundice and am yellow in the
face,' Shoola Pani says, peering at himself in the
bevelled mirror on the hat stand in the verandah.
He looks away, disgusted with himself. It's a habit
he will have to exorcise: the need to check himself
in a mirror each time he sees one.

Biju mumbles something, but Shoola Pani
swipes his thumb across the end call button on the
screen.

It has been only five days since he got here and already his life has fallen into a pattern that seems to iron out the creases of his being. Where is she? he wonders, looking at the little clock on the mantelpiece. Is it a working fireplace? He should ask her, he decides, and picks up his phone with the listed number.

You know what you are doing, don't you? he tells himself.

She picks up the phone after eight rings. It's the longest he has ever had to wait when he calls. Usually someone answers the phone on the third or fourth ring.

'I was just about to call you,' she says. And then, as though conscious of what she has said, a little breathless laugh.

'Oh, why?'

'I was wondering if you would like to come by for some coffee.' Her voice trails away uncertainly.

'I would,' he smiles into the phone. 'I don't think I've drunk as much coffee in my entire life as I have in the last two days.'

'Me too,' she giggles. Then, as if to interject a note of seriousness, she asks, 'Were you calling me for a specific reason?'

'Do I need a reason to call you?' he asks softly.

There is something liberating about not having to prevaricate. Over the years he has become the man he lets the camera see him as. The man everyone wants him to be. His only form of rebellion has been a cultivated surliness.

He hears her draw in a breath. He thinks it's the most erotic sound he has ever heard.

'But if you want one, I do,' he says. 'Is the fireplace usable?'

'Yes,' she says. 'Do you want me to come by and show you how to light a fire? I can get Muthu or John to bring you some firewood too.'

A silence falls between them.

'When will you come?'

'When do you want me to?'

They speak together.

He hears the hiss of her indrawn breath again.

'Soon,' she says in a fake-cheerful voice.

He wonders if her husband is in the room. 'Don't make it too late,' he says.

She puts the receiver down with a thudding heart. She has been married for almost sixteen years now and has never thought of herself as a woman who would look beyond her marriage.

She chose to marry KK because she wasn't in love with him. To love someone was to let them have power over you. She had seen her parents torture themselves and each other with this thing called love. She had known what it was to love and how it took away all semblance of sanity. And she had resolved that there was more to marriage than love. When you are not in love, how can you fall out of it? You can aspire to companionship, days in the golden wintery sun, threatened by neither scorching heat nor sudden rain clouds; you can make that yours and never worry that anything would change. The changeability of love terrified her.

But here she is, with a heart playing hopscotch: I am a wife. I have a life.

Will countless repetitions of saying it over and over again make a difference? Will it tame her thoughts and bind these feet that want to race to him?

Hayagriva – A few days after I came to work here, Leema's mother gave me a cookbook. She said its name was *Samayuthu Paar* and it was written by Meenakshiambal. I can't read or write, I said. Thus began our practice of discussing recipes. She taught me a great deal and now that Leema manages the home, I run the kitchen. Except that Leema seems to constantly urge me to try out new recipes she has discovered in magazines. The trouble with experiments is, we never know how they will turn out. If I see something turning into a disaster, I add a few things to salvage it. Leema is happy at the thought that I have mastered yet another dish she led me towards and I am happy that we didn't waste precious food. I suppose this must be what KK means by a win-win situation.

HAYAGRIVA

H

It is strange, I think, that in the Tamizh cuisine, we do not have a dish or an ingredient that begins with the sound H. I tell Leema that.

She is sitting at the kitchen table doing the weekly accounts. 'There is honey,' she says.

'Honey is an English word. Who says it except convent-educated girls like you? I call it thennu,' I say, standing at her elbow.

'What about halwa?' she asks.

I shake my head. 'It doesn't feel like an H,' I say.

'Are you serious?' She finally raises her head to look at me.

'I am,' I frown. 'I am too old to learn the English alphabet any other way but mine.'

She smiles and says, 'Come with me.'

'What's up?' KK asks as we walk towards the

table where he usually sits with his folding computer. It is a laptop, Leema has told me again and again, but in my head I call it a folding computer.

'We need to do a quick search,' she says.

Three minutes later, she has a name for me. Hayagriva.

'It sounds like an H, but what is it? That is important,' I say.

She smiles. 'It's the name of the horse-headed avatar of Vishnu.'

I like that. An H has to stand tall and not be a sloppy floppy mess solidified into a halwa. 'What about the dish?' I ask again.

She tilts her head back. You are going to need glasses soon, I think. As she reads the recipe aloud, I realize it's just a version of my bholi stuffing dressed in a skirt and blouse, with long dangling earrings to make it seem different.

Leema laughs when I say that. KK too. Sometimes he manages to find a smile for me. If only he would smile more often, I think.

'Sometimes we call a thing by a different name and tell ourselves it's something else even though we know the truth. We like to fool ourselves,' I say pointedly.

Leema's mouth tightens. KK looks away and I go off to make them hayagriva.

8

They stand by the grave with the fallen angel in the English cemetery. On the wall alongside the gate, ivy has grown, turning it into a wall of green. There are exactly eighteen graves there. 'In life and death, they kept themselves separate,' Lena says, running her hand along the shoulder of the fallen angel. 'When my grandfather bought the estate from the Englishman, he was made the custodian of the cemetery too.'

They walk from grave to grave, reading the headstones. Then she retraces her steps back to the fallen angel.

'I often wonder about her; this Jane Abigail Grey, born August 1891, died 3 October 1921, "beloved wife and mother". And what does this mean? "In Arcadia we shall meet and hold hands forever."' Lena's voice is wistful.

'Do you think he meant Arcadia as in Eden, or the golden age?' he says musingly.

She blinks in surprise. She didn't think he would know what it was that made her stand by the grave. Or what drew her to the fallen angel whose arms seemed to embrace the gravestone, her face tilted upwards imploringly.

'She must have left her home in England as a young woman and come here to make her own Arcadia. What would have made her follow a man? Do you think love alone could have? Look at the words inscribed: "I made me gardens and orchards and I planted trees in them of all kind of fruits. *Ecclesiastes* 2.5."'

He looks at her and murmurs, 'Thy plants are an orchard of pomegranates with pleasant fruits; camphire with spikenard.'

Lena's hand goes to her mouth in surprise. 'That's from the *Song of Solomon*. How do you know that?'

For a moment he debates with himself if he should come up with a line from one of his films. Over the years he has played countless variations of the man in love speaking words appropriate to just about every possible situation.

'I am an actor,' he says quietly. 'The *Song of Solomon* is a great favourite with screenplay writers in Malayalam. So I read it in English to understand it better. For some reason a few lines stayed etched in my head, refusing to blur or fade away.' He leans against a tree trunk as he speaks.

She gazes at his face. 'Thank you for being honest with me.'

'You think a lot about that each time I open my mouth, don't you?' he asks.

She flushes.

'I want you to know that what I said now was meant. Every word of it, Lee.' There, he had said her name.

'Lee?' Her eyes widen.

'She likes it!' His lips crinkle at the corners.

'She does indeed!'

I like Lee, she thinks. I like what the sound does for me. Why had no one called her Lee before?

'And what do I call you?' she asks.

He shrugs and says with a lazy smile, 'You'll figure it out. Does it matter? In Arcadia, names are irrelevant, Lee.'

She darts a quick look at him.

'No, that isn't a dialogue from one of my movies... I truly believe that. It's this sense of harmony you and I share.'

He holds out his hand to her and she takes it. Who moves first? Later they would tease each other about it. But in that moment, in that cemetery of forgotten graves and fallen angels, under a tree with dense green leaves, they embrace.

'Arcadia,' they say to each other. For how can anything that feels so perfect be anything less than the garden of Eden, the golden age, a world where everything but the two of them is irrelevant.

He feels it deep within him, a quietness that flows and heals, a warmth that melts each hardened knot of ennui, unravelling all the doubts.

She feels it too – runnels of energy that ignite dead tissue and numbed feelings; a fire that heals even as it flares within her.

They hold each other, unwilling to move, unwilling to even breathe, for to do so would be to step away from Arcadia.

Inji – One day, just after their wedding, as I served lunch, I heard Leema and KK talk. 'Do you think inji came from ginger or the other way around?' KK, who has a library in his head, gave her a long reply about how the word came from Samskrutham. I wanted to clang their heads together. Was this what newlyweds should be discussing? Couldn't she sidle up to him and give him a knowing look? Couldn't he pinch her cheek and whisper something in her ear?

iNJi

I

When Leema was a child, the fable of the fox and the grapes left her all confused and distressed. 'But Akka, why would the fox say the grapes are sour just because he couldn't reach them?' she would say again and again and I would wonder how this child was going to survive the real world when she didn't understand that it was all right to feel the slimy underbelly of emotions: resentment, envy, anger, pettiness, wrath...when we are human, we must allow ourselves all of it.

The girl who comes back from her walk has made a pact with some pagan force of nature. Her hair is windblown, her cheeks are rosy and she looks smug as the fox who got the grapes and found them sweet. Which is the grape? I wonder. The actor in the cottage or the feelings he seems to have aroused in her? Too much sweetness is going to cause her indigestion and addle her brains, I think with a snort. And decide, out of a sheer sense of perversity, to make some injikozhambu. A bit of inji in her system will pull her down from the clouds.

I also know that to serve this dish at lunch tomorrow, I must prepare it now. For injikozhambu needs to steep overnight. The heat of ginger, the tartness of tamarind and the aroma of spice need to wed during the night. I know it will put KK in a good mood. And if his mood is good, maybe he will bed his wife. Hopefully that will bring her down from the clouds even if the injikozhambu doesn't, and remind her of who she is.

As I slice the inji into strips, they remind me of a letter of the alphabet, but I can't remember which one. I rummage through the alphabet book and I see it: I.

Inji, I. I nod to myself. Will I ever forget what an I looks like? I don't think so.

And will Leema remember that even the sweetest of sweet grapes taste commonplace after a time? I don't think so.

9

He wakes up abruptly. Outside, the sky is still dark. There are no rain clouds to be seen, only stars. Perhaps the weather is about to break. He draws the quilt up to his chin and props an extra pillow under his head to see the skies better.

He cannot remember when he loved a place as much. The cream walls painted with a heavy hand, on which hang framed prints of flower paintings; the eccentric plumbing and dodgy wiring; the scampering feet of rats and squirrels in the false roof beneath the asbestos roofing; the chairs with sunken seats and the smoothness of the table he has appropriated for himself as his work station; the feel of the red oxide floor beneath his feet and the wild garden outside the cottage. He can hear the leaves rustle on the tree outside the window. When did he last know such a sense of oneness with the world around him, or himself?

The universe is a slab of frozen butter through which he slides, straight and unflinching, a heated knife that neither swerves nor stops. The golden butter moment, he thinks. He must tell Lee about it. In Arcadia, that must be how it is: a mellow golden light arcs on everything and there isn't a single shadow to mar the moment. Everything in its time and place, of its own volition.

A thought snags. Where is he going with this? How can he let her become so important to him? He feels his golden butter moment melt into a greasy puddle. He needs no one. He has never needed anyone. To let someone in would be to open the doors to weakness and the anguish of not knowing. Dread wears a black cloak, he knows, not death. We don't fear death; our fear of being abandoned is greater. On his pedestal he is unreachable and unassailable, but he has also known an emptiness nothing has ever been able to fill.

Everything he has done until now, the roles played, the accolades and applause won, the possessions accumulated, his marriage and children, everything became irrelevant the moment she and he stepped into Arcadia. Their Arcadia. Their golden butter moment.

He gets up from the bed and walks to the sitting room of the cottage. From a particular angle by the window, he can see a part of the main house and the window in that wall. He stands there, gazing and wondering.

※

Lena lifts the edge of the quilt and slips out of bed. The dogs curled up on a rug by the bed raise their heads. She pats them on the back and presses them down. 'Go back to sleep, boys,' she whispers. She glances at the clock on the wall in the corridor. It's a little past four. But she is wide awake and there is a singing in her veins. All of her, nerve ends and pores, opens up to the universe.

The dogs follow her with their eyes as she goes to the window and opens her arms out as if to draw all of it in – the starlit skies, the chill of the breeze, the rustle of the leaves on trees, the approaching dawn and, through it all, a nucleus of hope, comfort and solace. Him. She is still unable to think of a name for him. A name that will make him hers like Lee makes her his.

She looks at the man asleep on the bed. Her husband. He has an arm over his head. I've done you an injustice, she thinks. I thought it was enough that we were compatible. I thought complexities of emotion wouldn't endure and we would be left with the taste of chalk in our mouths. I thought it would be best to locate ourselves on a plateau of no expectations. But why didn't you want more? Why didn't you demand that I give you more?

She realizes that she cannot bear to be in the

same room that he is in. She walks to the parlour and switches on the lamp in the bay window. From where she stands, a part of the cottage is visible.

The Englishman had planned it so that, if he ever needed to signal to the overseer in his cottage, he could do so. No servant would step out with a message in the middle of the night.

As she watches, a light comes on in the window. He is there, she thinks. The exhilaration catches her unawares. How can it be that a light in a window can cause such headiness in her?

How can it be that the mere thought of him can fill me with such overwhelming joy? What is this thing that is happening to me?

And does he feel the same?

Jeera – Over the years, many things about me have changed, including my language. I became so much a part of that family that I started saying even Tamizh words as if they were Malayalam. I didn't realize how much the family and their ways had become a part of me until one day Leema said to me, 'Akka, it's funny that you say jeerakam like we say in Malayalam and not seerakam like in Tamizh.' I shrugged. 'I began saying it like Ammachi did, so that she would understand me, and after a while it became my way too. You can get used to anything after a while.'

JEERA

J

I don't know what to say. The truth is, I don't know what to think. Leema is in love. But she will never admit to it. She doesn't believe in love. There is duty, responsibility, there is tenderness, affection, lust even. But love is something we created to explain our erratic behaviour, she said to me, when I asked if she was in love with her KK the night before her wedding.

'This thing you call love...what has it done for you, Akka?' she asked. 'Two people saying you give me this and I will give you that in return. Like a barter.'

I tried to reason. 'You have the option to marry a man you love. I didn't have that. I couldn't even dream of it.'

But she wouldn't budge from this notion that it

was best to marry a man she didn't love rather than one she did. I don't know what happened to make her fear love as she does. When she was a child, her favourite candy wasn't toffee or chocolate but jeeramuttai. Sugar-coated jeera that came in little plastic tubes. Rainbow-coloured jeeramuttai that she would pop into her mouth after throwing her head back. I would see the incredulity in her eyes as the jeera filled her mouth. I never tired of watching her. Such joy over something so trivial. That's what love can be like, I wanted to tell her then. I wish I could tell her that now.

She is in the kitchen when I go in, sipping green tea from a mug. How she can drink what seems like hot water is beyond me!

'Good morning,' she says.

'Namaste,' I say. 'I have something to ask you.'

Her head jerks up.

'Jeerakam, how do you spell it? With a g or a j?'

She laughs. 'With a J. Do you remember the jeeramuttai you used to buy me?'

I lean forward and tuck a strand of her hair behind her ear. 'I remember. I thought you had forgotten.'

'Why do you say that?'

'That look in your eyes as you crunched a mouthful of jeeramuttai… I don't see it any more. That's why,' I retort.

10

She walks to the market square with him. 'Ah, the piazza,' he smiles. He had spent forty-five days shooting in various parts of Italy for a new film.

'We call it mattom,' she says with a laugh. 'That means empty.'

'I know,' he drawls. 'I speak Tamizh just as well as you do! Better, in fact!'

He looks at the stone-paved square hemmed in by whitewashed buildings with blue doors and windows. In the late morning light, the white walls glow. He stands at the end of the road and studies the scene. 'It's like a movie set,' he says. 'Perhaps I should suggest it as a possible location.'

She feels some of the glow fade. The very thought of his other life is like biting on a mouthful of grit.

'But what have we come here for?' he asks.

She narrows her eyes and clenches her jaw. 'I'll be back,' she says in her best Arnold Schwarznegger voice, walking ahead to the shop that sells groceries, vegetables, biscuits, buckets, brooms, ropes and mosquito coils.

When she comes back, she's wearing a large smile. She holds up two clear plastic tubes crammed with multi-coloured sugar-coated cumin. 'Remember these?' she asks. There is an impish glint in her eyes.

'Oh my god!' His laugh erupts like a bark of joy. 'The last time I ate jeeramuttai, I must have been thirteen, I think.'

She gives him a tube. He tears open one end and squeezes the contents into his mouth. She watches his face as the sugar-coated cumin come alive in his mouth. She wonders what it would be like to kiss him. What am I thinking? she tells herself and strides ahead.

He follows her, wondering about the sudden change of expression on her face, the abrupt dipping of temperature between them.

'Why do you like the English cemetery so much?' he asks, seeing where they we are headed.

She shrugs. 'Do I need a reason?'

He doesn't speak. They walk in silence. He watches her walk towards the grave with the fallen angel.

'What's wrong?' he asks, turning her towards him.

'I don't know,' she whispers. 'I don't know what is happening.' She raises her face towards his, leans forward and kisses him.

Her lips on his are delicate as a moth's wing. He draws in his breath. 'I didn't see that coming!'

He sees a shadow cloud her eyes. 'Lee, what I meant was, I didn't know…' And then, knowing words are superfluous to this thing between them, this thing that has no name, he pulls her towards him.

The kiss. Have they ever known such an intimate exploration of another person with a mere touch of the lips? She goes up on her toes. There are inches separating them; almost a lifetime. The missing years, the separate lives; all of it had to be conjoined in this first kiss.

'Stand on my shoes,' he murmurs. He feels her smile against his lips.

'Won't it hurt your toes?'

'No,' he says and parts her mouth with his.

They meld into each other. His hands curve around her buttocks. She slips her hands beneath his shirt and splays her fingers on the skin of his back. She tastes the cumin in his mouth. He tastes the sugar in hers.

'I could do this forever,' he says, raising her chin.

'I know,' she says.

He pulls her even closer, until he can feel all of her against him.

Her breath catches in her throat. He buries his face in the curve of her neck.

'Oh my Lee, what are we going to do?' he mumbles against her skin.

She winds her arms around his neck tightly. 'I don't know… All I know is, I don't want to ever let go.'

Over her head he sees the fallen angel. It has a knowing look.

Karuvepillai – I am told the English word curry came from karuvepillai, which some red-in-the-face Dorai or Missy fanning themselves silly after a meal of curry and rice thought was what went into a curry. There is some truth in that, for without karuvepillai a curry isn't complete. You would think that something we require everyday in our cooking would grow rampantly. But it isn't easy to grow karuvepillai. It is a plant that refuses to be planted; it has to grow on its own terms. It likes to travel in a bird's belly and be shat out and then, if it likes the soil, the colour, the texture, the wetness, the crumbly nature of the top soil, the plants growing nearby, the family history of the earthworms and beetles, this whimsical seed will root itself and put forth a seedling. Does it stop there? The karuvepillai grows at its own pace; you can't water or manure it and hasten its growth. So everyone treated the karuvepillai plant with such care until there came a day when the karuvepillai thought itself to be the centre of the universe.

KARUVEPiLLAi

K

I place the long-handled iron spoon on the stove. I need to season the chutney for the idlis I have made for breakfast. It is a chutney with coconut and broken gram. I like it better than plain coconut; the nuttiness of the gram adds a certain fillip to it. I watch as the mustard seeds splutter. I add karuvepillai. The oil hisses and the kitchen is filled with an aroma that only karuvepillai can release.

I smile to myself. I had thought a lot about how I was going to remember the letter K, but now I know that K can only be Karuvepillai. A leaf we can't do without, in just about anything we cook. Like salt, karuvepillai brings alive every dish it is added to. In fact, like salt, no kitchen is complete without it.

But karuvepillai is not a woman's friend. If we

touch it on the days we bleed, it will dry up. It will not dry up if a man who beats his wife, starves his mother or rapes a two-year-old girl goes near it. That is how karuvepillai is. It is said that a goddess tried to talk the karuvepillai out of this disdain for women and the course of nature but it has such pride of place in the kitchen that it wouldn't heed even a goddess's words.

So, as if to punish it for not understanding that a woman will bleed and must not be treated like an unclean creature during that period, the goddess cursed the karuvepillai for such pride: without a woman you will have no importance. But since you feel you cannot acknowledge her, warts, blood and all, you will be left on the side of the plate, to be tossed out with the debris of a meal: stalks, bones, pips and suchlike.

Which is why we refer to someone who is discarded after use as a karuvepillai.

Leema would do well to remember that. Actors like him will use people. They get to where they are only because they don't let anything hold them back or down.

11

'That actor, he's an odd sort of fellow,' KK says, buttering his toast carefully, precisely one centimetre away from the crust. Lena looks up from her idiappam and egg curry.

'Not odder than you are,' she mumbles softly.

'Why do you think I am odd?' KK frowns.

'We have one of the best cooks in what must be all of Tamil Nadu and you still want to eat toast and porridge for breakfast. Don't you think that's odd?' Lena spoons a dollop of curry onto her plate.

KK makes a face. 'Can't help it. Twelve years of boarding-school breakfast!'

'I went to boarding school too, KK,' Lena says with a flash of irritation.

'Yes, but you know me, Lena, I am a creature of habit,' KK says as he peels an orange and breaks it into neat segments.

'Am I just a habit to you, KK?' Lena asks quietly.

'What a ridiculous thing to say! You are my wife, Lena.' He pops a segment of orange into his mouth and chews. Someone once told him that it was advisable to chew every mouthful thirty-two times.

Lena wonders how anyone who sounds so reasonable can make her want to empty a tureen of egg curry over his head. Even if she does, he'll reach for the boiled egg precariously resting on the top of his head, wipe it clean with a tissue and eat it with as much enjoyment as if she had served it to him in an egg cup. There is no riling KK.

'Why do you think he is odd?' Lena asks, twirling strands of idiappam around her finger.

'Don't play with your food,' he says.

Lena glares at him. 'When did you become my father?'

He sighs. Then, as if to change the subject, he says in that reasonable voice of his that sets her teeth on edge, 'Well, have you seen him standing on the edge of the cliff?' I wonder what he is thinking as he stands there... He has come here for a break, I am told. Why would a successful actor like him need a break?'

Lena doesn't speak as she watches KK rise from the dining table. She wonders at how he seems to be able to produce on demand that tone of voice.

She first met KK at a friend's home in Chennai. His parents had been teachers in Uganda. They had to flee in the last years of Idi Amin's regime. KK was at boarding school in Mussoorie then.

They had found teaching positions in Zambia and had ultimately migrated to Canada. But KK's life had remained untouched. Boarding school was home and its traditions his. It taught him an equanimity which had drawn Lena to him. The cool young lawyer who never got drunk and was the last man standing at every party while the rest of the men became either maudlin or rambunctious or quarrelsome. Nothing seemed to move him to extremes on the emotional barometer. Lena, who feared all emotional excess, saw in him the stillness of a pond. And now she thinks it is this ability she resents the most. He knows exactly how to talk her out of anything. He knows the right buttons to press, to clamp her wildest thoughts and turn her into the woman she has trained herself to be. Kind. Reasonable. Dignified. And dead as a doormat, she thinks.

'I like him,' she says defiantly.

'You and most of the under-forty female population of south India,' KK laughs. 'I still can't get over the fact that instead of consolidating his career, he has chosen to hide himself here.'

Lena rises from the table. She goes to the living-room bay window from where she can see his cottage. What is he doing now? she wonders. What is he thinking of? And then: who is he thinking of? Lena feels a sourness in her mouth; the taste of an egg gone bad.

What is happening to her? At parties, when KK dances with other women or flirts with girls half his age, she usually watches in amusement. His silver streaked hair against his deep brown skin, his chiselled features and his taut leanness make him attractive to most women. She has seen how he has them eating out of his hands within minutes of talking to them. KK is an incorrigible flirt and she has never resented how he uses his charm to gather women around him.

She knows it's foolish of her to read more than mere attraction into what she feels for Shoola Pani. Ships in the night, that's what they are. Each with a course to follow and separate ports of call. And yet, the very thought of Shoola Pani thinking of another woman makes her want to retch.

She closes her eyes and leans against the window.

'Are you all right?' KK asks.

She nods, sitting down.

Laddoo – Whoever first thought of making laddoo couldn't have had much of an imagination. Among all our sweets, the shaping of a laddoo is probably the easiest. You take a handful of whatever, rava, boondi or kadalamavu, coconut or pori, and roll into balls. Not like jangery, which requires a deft hand, or even mysore pak that needs to be poured into a plate and sliced, or badushah, which needs to be crimped. But does it really matter how a sweet is shaped? When you bite into it, all that carefully constructed beauty falls apart. What you remember is not how it looked but how it tasted. A square laddoo would taste just as good as a round one. But what do I know? If I were to tell someone this, they would only say that I can't make proper round-round laddoos and so I am making excuses for myself. It's the same about life. If we want to live our time on this planet differently from what is the accepted way, they mock you and make you feel you have done nothing that matters. Such is life and the making of laddoos.

LADDOO

L

He seems to be in a good mood. He has brought a box of laddoos from Coimbatore. 'What's the occasion?' I ask.

'Can't I buy a box of laddoos for no reason?' KK laughs.

I like that. Women like that in a man. An impulsive gesture.

'I know how much you like sweets,' he adds, and then whispers with a secret smile, 'but don't tell your Leema. She says you can't have sugar or oil.'

I shrug. 'Leema isn't always right.' I see the look of surprise in his eyes. He has never heard me speak a word against her. I hasten to add, 'Even if she means well.'

His mouth twists into a grimace. 'Don't I know that?'

What does he know? Even if he does, he won't speak his thoughts.

'Have one,' I say, feeling a wave of pity for him.

He meets my eye and grins. 'I already ate two at the shop. I don't need a reason to eat a sweet.'

It isn't easy to understand him, I think.

When he leaves the kitchen, I look at the box of laddoos. He is right. We only make sweets as part of a celebration. Why don't we ever do it to make ourselves happy? Do we women value ourselves so little?

A laddoo looks nothing like a 'L', but some streak of cussedness makes me decide that my L will be a round laddoo. Just as one shouldn't need a reason to pop a sweet into one's mouth, I tell myself, as I take a large bite of a laddoo. It's delicious.

Once upon a time I could make laddoos. I would add a pinch of camphor and cloves. It would balance the sweetness and add a dash of divinity as if, with a laddoo, you were entering a temple. In fact, for Leema's first wedding anniversary, I made two hundred laddoos. But my laddoo-making days are over. I can never get it right any more.

I have heard other women say this as well. But never a male cook. Why is it we lose our ability to cook as we age? Along with our fecundity, do we lose our ability to create too? Men somehow seem to age better. Why is that? I wonder.

And so I bite into my second laddoo. For now it makes me happy. Besides, why would I want to sweat over a hot stove making laddoos when they can be bought?

12

She hears voices. A female and two male voices.

She pauses at his doorstep. She had noticed the jeep parked next to his car but didn't really think about it. He had said a director friend of his might drive up to see him.

Should she go back, she wonders as she stands uncertainly at the end of the gravel path.

The door opens and a man steps out. He looks at her blankly. Then Shoola Pani appears in the doorway. He looks furious, but his expression switches to one of tenderness when he sees her. The consummate actor, she thinks, uneasily.

'Come in,' he says, holding the door wide open for her.

She sees a woman seated in the chair she has begun to think of as hers. And on the sofa, a hapless-looking man.

'This is Biju, my secretary,' Shoola Pani says. 'And this is Renuka Joshi, a very talented film-maker.'

Leema takes in the young woman with her swirly skirt, short-sleeved blouse, silver jewellery, ankle boots and perfectly coiffured hair on top of which a pair of sunglasses sits. She looks more like an actress, a starlet, she thinks almost cattily.

'This is Lena. This cottage is hers,' he says.

A taloned hand claws within her. What did she expect? That he would proclaim what she means to him? But what is her place in his life anyway?

'So will you think about it, sir?' the young woman asks.

'Hmm,' he mumbles and then, turning to Lena, he points to the box she is clutching in her hand. 'What is that?' he asks.

'Laddoos. KK brought a box back and I thought you might like a few,' she says, offering it to him.

He opens it and takes one.

'Sir, you shouldn't be eating sweets,' Biju says in an unhappy voice.

'Are you diabetic?' Lena asks, wondering if that's why he seems to not put on weight at all.

'No,' he says, popping the laddoo whole into his mouth.

The film-maker and Biju exchange glances.

'It's not about being diabetic. The camera adds inches and that isn't good for his image,' Biju explains.

'Don't talk about me as if I am not in the room,' Shoola Pani says with his mouth full.

He wipes the crumbs from around his mouth and dusts his palms on the sides of his track pants.

Lena sees horror flash on Biju's face. The film-maker looks more bemused than horrified. This is the man who is never seen in public with a hair out of place.

'Shouldn't you be going?' Shoola Pani asks pointedly, moving towards the door. 'It's a long drive back to Pollachi and from there to Chennai.'

Renuka Joshi gets up even if Biju seems reluctant to do so. 'But sir, we got here just forty-five minutes ago,' he says in a mutinous tone.

'Yes, and I think we have discussed everything we need to.' Shoola Pani's voice is glacial.

'When should I come back?' Biju persists.

Shoola Pani frowns. 'I'll let you know.'

The man who had walked out earlier is standing by the jeep, talking into his mobile.

'That's a financier. Biju brought him to lure me back. I threw him out,' Shoola Pani murmurs into her ear. She sees Renuka hop into the driving seat and reverse the vehicle smoothly. The two men clamber in.

Lena nibbles on her lip. What can she offer this man? She has neither a career nor talent. She isn't beautiful or clever. She can't even drive. What does he see in her? Is she anything more than a mere diversion? Once again, the disconcerting image she has of them: ships in the night.

'Are you happy, Lee?' he asks.

She looks at his face. Something twists within her. 'I am happy, Ship,' she says finally, landing on a name for him.

'Ship?' His mouth wobbles in amusement.

She grins. 'Yes. That's your name. Ship. So, are you happy, Ship?'

There is a sweetness that surrounds them. The innocence of two children on their own, discovering a secret garden they hadn't known about. A secret garden that is just theirs.

'What did she want?' she asks. It is in the nature of Eve to allow the serpent to coil within her and hiss in her ear.

'Renuka? She's a bright young film-maker... She has an amazing script and, who knows, the film could even make it to Cannes,' he says.

What did she expect of him? That he would stay here and never leave?

Murungakai – Just outside my aachi's home was a murungakai tree that bore fruit throughout the year. Every few days a young woman from the neighbouring street, whose elderly husband played the thavil, came by to pluck a few. When I was a child I thought that she dried the murungakai for her husband to use to beat his drum. Aachi and some of the neighbouring women hid their faces behind their palms and giggled when I asked her why she didn't ask her husband to make a stick out of wood. She wouldn't need to almost kill herself by climbing the murungakai tree every week to pluck the fruit. She sighed and said I wouldn't understand. A year later, she ran away with a steel utensil vendor. What will he do for the drumstick now? I asked aachi, worried for him. Aachi almost choked as she said, 'Don't you worry about that. The poor man must be relieved to be left alone!' A few months later, his new wife was on the tree, plucking drumsticks for her husband. And I was at peace, knowing that he wouldn't have to give up being a drummer. What did I know? I was only a seven-year-old girl!

MURUNGAKAI

M

Leema is in a chatty mood. She wants to know about my husband who was a Karagam dancer.

'What was it like to be married to him?'

'I wasn't really,' I tell her wryly. 'He was more often away than with me. I saw him once every few weeks. At first I hated it when he left. But after a while I got used to it. In fact, I found his being at home a nuisance.'

She examines her fingernails. KK spends a great deal of time away from home. It doesn't seem to bother either of them. So she surprises me when she asks, 'Did you ever wonder what he did when he was away?' She continues to examine her fingernails.

'All the time, at first, and then I stopped.'

Her head shoots up. 'Why?'

I tell her the truth.

'My fear that he would leave me for another woman made my mouth taste bitter all the time. It made me angry and scared when we were together. I was constantly looking for a sign of the other woman. She was more real to me than to him until, one day, it struck me that I would drive him into another woman's bed.'

Leema has a strange expression as she says, 'So it was another woman's bed you were worried about; not that he may just want to be with her.'

I am chopping murungakai as we talk. I see that she has taken the chopped pieces as long as my little finger and made an alphabet out of them. M. I have my M, I think.

'Don't underestimate the importance of what a man and woman do together in bed...or on the floor or the garden bench.' I smile, thinking of my Rayar.

I had cooked a murungakai sambhar that day. The aroma filled the kitchen and spread to the rest of the house. Rayar heaped his plate with rice and I ladled sambhar over the steaming rice. He picked up a murungakai piece between his thumb and forefinger and sucked on it slowly. I felt the tug on my nipples.

'Do you know what this does?' he smiled, holding my gaze. I felt like I was falling down a tunnel.

I shook my head. When I was with him, I turned into a young girl.

'It makes a man want to do things to a woman he is drawn to.'

My gaze dropped. I felt shy and aroused at the same time. I knew then that we would make love.

Everyone was away that night. He came to my room. He stood at the door and devoured me with his eyes.

The murungakai enhances the libido, they say. I don't know if it does or doesn't. But nothing arouses a woman more than knowing a man desires her, as if she's a fever in his blood.

My poor Leema, I think. All this education and wealth, so much of everything in her life, but has her KK ever looked at her as if she were a fever in his blood?

For lunch I am going to make murungakai sambhar. Maybe it will do something to KK. Maybe he will finally treat her like a woman.

13

Lena gnaws at her lower lip as she walks towards the crèche. At breakfast KK asked her if she had forsaken the crèche. There was neither condemnation nor censure in his voice, but precisely for that reason, Lena felt guilty. 'The children were asking for you, one of the ayahs said, when they came to the factory last evening to collect the weekly rations.'

Most mornings, Lena is at the crèche. She has drawn up diet, medical and activity charts to ensure that the children are well looked after. She never stays away from the crèche unless she is travelling or unwell. Most mornings she is there from nine to eleven before setting out on her walk. But she hasn't been to the crèche in a week now. Ever since he came to stay, all her mornings have been spent with him. The walk is their pretext, their reason to be together. In the evenings she drops in with a tray of food but she doesn't stay for long. He watches her leave with a forlorn expression that both saddens her and fills her with a heady exhilaration.

He is waiting by the bridge. 'What's wrong?' he asks, seeing the confusion in her eyes.

'I haven't been to the crèche for some days now,' she says.

'Crèche?' His eyebrows rise.

She smiles. 'We started it almost ten years ago. The female workers with toddlers stayed away from work, not knowing what to do. But with the crèche they had somewhere to leave the children when they went out to the fields. The ayahs cook the children's food, which I taste before it's given to the children. I teach them songs and rhymes and the older ones are given colouring books.'

'Nice,' he says.

'So that means we can't go walking as we do.' Her eyes drop. She wonders how she'll survive the day if she doesn't wrap her arms around his neck and lay her cheek against his chest.

'Shall I join you?' he asks.

'Will you, Ship?'

Her eyes light up, and he feels a rush of triumph. Which man wouldn't, when the woman he is drawn to sparkles at the mere mention of them being together?

They walk down the road towards the mattom. A little lane to the left leads to the crèche. It is an old building with white-washed walls and a high gabled roof laid with asbestos sheets. The windows and doors are painted a brilliant kingfisher blue and around the building is a line of flowering shrubs.

An avocado tree casts a pool of shadow over the play area with its sandpit, a see-saw and two swings. A toddler sits in the sandpit, pouring sand from one plastic cup to another. 'That's Dulari,' Lena says. 'I'm not sure what's wrong with her, but the doctor who comes in once a month thinks she may be autistic. She doesn't join the rest of the children. It's like she's in her own world.'

The children rush to the stable doors as they see Lena walk up the path. 'Aunty, aunty,' they clamour in loud excited voices, their hands stretching over the half-open door. How could she have stayed away for so long? Lena and Shoola Pani exchange a glance. She smiles at him almost in embarrassment, at the effusiveness of the children. The children look at him curiously but it is her they focus on. Lena feels a tug on her tunic. She turns to see Dulari standing behind her. The child's face is blank and she is staring at the ground. She has her two cups with her, one of which is filled with sand. Lena's eyes fill.

It's strange, he thinks, to be of no consequence to a group of people. Everywhere he goes, there is always someone gazing at him with the wide-eyed wonder of having met a god in the flesh. But to these children, Lee is that miracle and he is just an appendage, perhaps an irritant even.

He watches as she settles on the low wooden platform while the children bustle around her. A girl crawls into her lap. Another one tries to push her away. Dulari sits on the floor, unwilling to be separated from Lena, and pours sand from one cup to the other. One of the ayahs rushes to take the sand cups away but Lena holds her hand up. 'Let her be for now,' she says.

That's when the ayah sees him. For the next few minutes, there is much excited giggling and the ayahs want to take a picture with him on their cell phones.

'At least they won't post it on Facebook,' Shoola Pani murmurs to Lena.

She smiles. 'Don't be so sure. But I'll tell them they mustn't.'

He shrugs, 'It's fine... The world is going to catch up with me sooner or later.'

'Children, say good morning to Uncle,' she says when they have finally arranged themselves around her to their satisfaction.

'Good morning, Uncle,' the children chorus obediently.

'I could be their grandfather,' he says wryly.

She looks at him in surprise. 'How old are you?' she asks.

He looks at her and smiles. 'Fifty-three.'

She doesn't conceal her surprise. 'I didn't know. You don't look it.'

'Yes, I was probably in college by the time you got into nursery school,' he says quietly.

'Does it matter?' she asks, picking up a brush and beginning to comb out a child's tangled curls.

He shrugs. 'Nothing matters.'

Except that you and I are here, they both think, and allow it to show in their eyes.

Nande – Each time we bought crabs at my aachi's home, it was a matter of much celebration. For they were both toys and food. We would try to catch them as they scurried across the cement floor of the backyard. The boys always managed to grab them. I was too afraid of the giant claws which looked like they would snap my fingers in two. We had crab races. But it didn't matter which crab won or lost, for they all ended up in the same pot. Dead. And we feasted on them and it didn't matter if the crab was a winner or a loser. They all tasted the same. Delicious.

NANDE

N

Muthu turns up with an earthen pot with a narrow mouth. It looks like the kind toddy tappers use, but here in the hills, where could he have found a toddy tapper? Or, for that matter, a coconut or palmyra tree?

'What's this?'

He grins at the suspicious note in my voice. 'Nande,' he says.

'From where?' I ask, for the sea is at least a hundred kilometres away.

'Madam wanted me to get it. So I told Ramesh, the driver of the Chalakudi bus, to organize it,' he says with the air of a man who has procured an impossibility, like an elephant's egg. 'It's fresh. Still alive,' he says, pushing aside the cloth wound around the mouth of the pot and peering in.

I frown. How am I supposed to kill the creatures? It's been years since I cooked them. And what's with Leema and this sudden craving for nande?

Muthu opens the mouth of the pot and pours the contents on the ground. Crabs jostle out and crawl sideways. I smile, seeing their gait. It's that actor's trademark on screen, even though he doesn't walk like that for real. I can see the makings of a private joke between them and it fills me with both tenderness and trepidation for her, my precious girl, Leema.

When a man and a woman start having a private language, things will soon get out of hand. It ceases to be just lust then: it becomes a matter of the heart. Or the liver, as Leema's mother believed it to be.

Things begin to fall into place. I think of all her questions: about men and performers, husbands and love affairs. About things we have never discussed before.

I watch Muthu pick up a crab and deftly prise open the outer shell. I flinch and look away. The violence of it unnerves me.

There is nothing like a delicious nandekari, but while one is cooking, one mustn't think of what came before and what will be left after.

There is no compassionate way to kill a crab.

You either boil it alive or dismember it even as it tries to crawl away. And when you are done, the debris litters the plate and table, the juices are splattered on your clothes, and around your mouth is a faint tingling of the skin from the spices and the abrasions caused by the shell as you bit down on a claw or sucked the flesh from within.

That is how it is with love. With my Rayar I never thought of who or what I was. When it was over, the debris left a stench that still lives within me. I wonder if Leema knows what it is to live with a part of your soul dead and decaying within. There is no escaping it till you are dead.

As Muthu grabs another nande, I have my letter N. Nande. The crab that will take you down with it and never let you get away.

14

'I have a surprise for you,' she says, proffering a covered dish.

He narrows his eyes and smiles at the same time. And her heart skips a beat. It's one of those expressions that he has used to great effect on the screen. No one else does it as well as he does.

He takes the dish from her. 'Muthu already came in with my dinner. What is this?'

Lena has prevailed upon KK to hire Muthu to fetch and carry stuff from the main house to the cottage and to keep the cottage and the grounds around it tidy. Komathi, she has noticed, seems to like having someone apart from Rosie to boss over. And each night, on his way home, Muthu drops off the dinner tray.

Except she now wishes she hadn't thought of hiring a helper. With Muthu on call, there is no reason for her to pop into the cottage. 'What are we paying that lay about for?' KK said once and added, 'Unless, of course, you want to. Star-struck fan, is it?'

She turned still at the tone of his voice. What was he implying? What was he thinking? Close on the heels of 'the children at the crèche are missing you', it seemed like an admonition.

KK seldom questioned what she did or intruded on her day. It seemed, in his quiet way, he was doing so now.

'Are you crazy? Trudging with a heavy tray three times a day… I only go there to make sure that Muthu is doing his job all right. It's the first time he is playing batman after all.' She smiled.

'Trudging with a tray three times a day…nice alliteration!' KK grinned. Then, another insidious question: 'Are you writing poetry again?'

'Poetry? Why?'

'You used to once…' he said and turned back to his packing. He was going to Chennai. 'I should be back in three or four days. Depending on how the hearing goes and the meetings thereafter.'

Lena waited for Muthu to leave before filling a tureen with the nandekari kozhambu. She felt Komathi's eyes on her as she set the tureen on a tray.

'Why didn't you send it with Muthu?' she sighed before Komathi could comment.

Who is this new me? Lena asked herself as she walked in the dusk towards Mimosa cottage. But it all seemed worthwhile – the deceit and duplicity,

the cunning and manipulation, the shards of guilt –
as she saw his eyes light up at the sight of her on his
doorstep.

There is a slight awkwardness between them.
The kiss at the English cemetery hovers. Does he
regret it? she wonders.

Does she? he wonders.

'You are good with kids,' he says softly.

She smiles wistfully.

'But you didn't have any of your own?'

'I was pregnant once. An ectopic pregnancy. It
messed up my insides. I can't have any of my own.'

'Are you all right?' he asks, seeing something
fade in her eyes.

'I should be going,' she says.

'Why? What's wrong, Lee?' he asks.

She shakes her head.

'Are you happy, Lee?' he asks.

She smiles. This is something she had begun.
Asking him every now and then: Are you happy,
Ship?

And he would answer: Am happy. Are you happy,
Lee?

And she would reply: Am happy, Ship.

She nods.

'No, you are not.' He looks at her carefully. 'I
can see that. What's wrong?'

'Just hold me,' she murmurs, walking towards him. He drops into a chair and pulls her into his lap. He rests his head on her breasts and she wraps her arms around his neck. They cradle one another. What would it be like if they didn't have each other? The prospect of loneliness makes them cling.

Oorkai – Can you imagine a kitchen without jars of oorkai? Mangoes or limes floating in a lake of oil and spice, made before the summer reaches its peak. So I was surprised when I came to this household and found they bought their pickles. 'Don't you make your own?' I asked Leema's mother. She shrugged. Ammachi used to make beef and fish pickle. But it's too much of an effort, she said. Soon I began making the pickles and Leema's daddy started finishing the food on his plate. Who would have thought a manga thokku would make such a difference?

OORKAI

O

I walk listlessly through the house. Leema has left the TV on for me to watch a Tamizh serial. But these sagas of mothers-in-law and daughters-in-law behaving like cats and dogs bore me. In fact, if I ever meet the director of one of these serials, I have every intention of giving him a good talking-to. What on earth are these idiots thinking, planting such nonsense in the minds of women?

My daughter-in-law Revathi and I get along well enough. I can never replace her mother and she will never be my daughter. If we can understand that and work within those boundaries, there will be no hiss or splutter.

Leema has taken a tureen of the nandekari kozhambu and gone off to the cottage. She said she would return quickly. But I doubt it. I understand these things even if she doesn't.

I switch off the TV and come back to the kitchen. The smell of the nandekari still hangs heavy. I put the dish away in the fridge. When Rosie comes in the morning, I will have her scour the kitchen.

I don't know why the smell of the nande bothers me so much. I have never found it so distasteful before. Perhaps because KK is away and she is there. Perhaps because I can already smell the stench of the debris that will be left when this madness is over.

I see the narthanga on the tray. Muthu must have plucked it before the monkeys got to it. They don't eat the bitter oranges but they will still pluck them and hurl them on the ground. I think I know what to do to clear the air in my kitchen. I will make oorkai out of narthanga.

The narthanga is like an O. Oorkai will be my O.

There are rules and rules about making oorkai. You mustn't make it on a Sunday, Tuesday or Friday. You must make it before the moon disappears entirely behind the clouds on an Amavasya night. You can't touch the oorkai when you are menstruating. You can't touch the pickle pot after being with a man. I don't set store by all that rubbish. My only rule when it comes to oorkai is that there should be no moisture or heating once the tempering of the oil is done.

Sometimes we must make our own rules, depending on what works for us. Which is why I don't understand myself. When Leema is making her own rules, why do I find myself unable to accept or approve?

15

He murmurs against her, 'I could stay here forever.'

'Umm…' she whispers into the skin of his neck.

'I was watching you with the children and I so wanted to be one of them,' he says.

She tilts his chin up so she can look into his eyes. 'Why?'

'The way you tickled them and made them laugh, the way you baby-talked them…' There is a wistfulness in his voice.

She presses his eyelids down and drops a kiss on them. The tenderness that fills her makes her want to weep. She doesn't understand it, except that there is a great sadness that envelops her. More to dissipate it than anything else, she leans away and growls, 'So be prepared to be tickled?'

He looks at her sidelong with a smirk. 'I'm not ticklish.'

'Really?'

'Really!'

'How can anyone not be ticklish?' She widens her eyes.

'Haven't you heard what they say about me? That I am cold, unfeeling and insensitive?' he smiles.

'Give me your hand,' she says.

'Don't tell me you read palms?'

She takes his palm in hers. She places her elbow in the middle of his palm and rotates it, speaking to him as if he were five and not fifty-three: 'Dig dig dig, I dug the ground.'

She folds his fingers one by one and continues in a theatrical whisper, 'I planted a banana tree. I watered it. A flower bloomed. The bananas appeared. But oh oh, what is this? Someone stole it!'

She looks at his amused face and then, rolling her eyes, opens out his fingers one by one, demanding: 'Did you see who did it? Did you see who did it? Did you see who did it? Did you see who did it?'

At the little finger, she pauses and, in a tinny voice, she squeaks, 'Yes, I did… I saw him run this way.'

'He ran this way, you say?' She uses her index and middle finger to drum her way up his arm till she reaches his shoulder and then with a note of triumph, she cries, 'Found him.' And then her fingers dart into his armpit to tickle him.

He bursts into laughter. 'Oh darling, Lee.'

She looks at his face, the child-like glow.

'Oh, Ship,' she says, murmuring nonsensical words in his ear. Sounds and syllables only a little child or an animal would respond to.

He nuzzles her neck with suppressed laughter. 'What is that?'

'Baby talk… Don't you know what that is, Mr Movie Star?'

He shakes his head. 'No one has ever baby-talked me before.'

She holds her breath. How can any mother not baby-talk a child? She thinks of her grandmothers and her parents, Akka and all the workers in the estate… They had swathed and suffocated her with their cooing, kissing, caressing and tickling.

She wraps her arms around him and cradles him as she murmurs, 'Loo li la la…njunju…'

Paavakai – I wonder what that pannaiyar God was thinking of when he created paavakai. Ugly to look at, with bumps and ridges, and bitter to the taste. Whoever reached for a paavakai at the vegetable shop because they want to? It usually is, 'I suppose this is good for me, so I must eat it at least once a week.' I don't care for it either way. I don't love it or hate it. But that's how I have become. Both love and hatred draw from the same reservoir of strength. And I have just enough to sustain me through the day without frittering it on hating and loving vegetables.

PAAVAKAi

P

I glance at the clock. It's a little past eight. More than an hour since she left.

My oorkai is cooling in the cast-iron cauldron. I'll bottle it tomorrow. There's nothing for me to do but wait as my oorkai does.

A bitterness fills my mouth. It isn't the sweet bitterness of the nellikai. This is more like the bitterness that fills your mouth when food sits as a lumpen mess in your intestines or rancour fills your heart.

I walk listlessly, feeling a cold knot of anger gather within me. I look at the vegetable bin that is kept in the corner of the kitchen. I see the crocodile-like ridges of the paavakai.

When Leema was a child, she used to think that the paavakai were baby crocodiles that we had trapped from the river and refused to eat them. She was a picky eater. Then one day I found out how I could use the paavakai to persuade her to eat. I stuck two bits of red chilli on one end of the paavakai to resemble eyes and pierced four matchsticks to suggest limbs. I made growling noises, threatening to eat her up if she didn't finish everything that was on her plate.

When she was older, she wasn't so easy to convince. The paavakai became a vegetable that filled her with horror. Its bitterness was unpalatable. But now it's one of her favourite vegetables. She eats it with the relish the rest of the world reserves for potatoes or brinjal.

The paavakai begins with a P. So does paal.

Give Leema a glass of milk with Horlicks and she will drink it to the last drop and scoop out the lumps at the bottom of the glass with a spoon. Give her a glass of paavakai juice and she will drain it to the last drop too. That is how contrary she is.

The paavakai is a peculiar vegetable. Bitter, yes. Yet, when you cook it in a cast-iron frying pan, roasting it over a low fire while drizzling oil from the sides, it caramelizes with a hint of crunchy sweetness. Or even a pinch of jaggery helps. But Leema will not let me cook it that way. She likes it just barely cooked. KK hates it, saying that he feels his mouth turning bitter just by looking at it.

That is my Leema, wanting to embrace bitterness of her own volition.

I peer out of the window. The mist has thickened into a fog. I cannot see the cottage any more.

I go to bed after locking up.

16

He suggested she stay for dinner. 'You can't just abandon me and go,' he said.

She agreed. There was no reason for her to rush back either. They ate, making little conversation. It was impossible to converse while eating crabs. Instead, the silence was punctuated by cracking and sucking sounds. And now, having cleared up and tidied the table, he lights an aromatic candle to remove the fug of crab and spice. They sit across from each other in a silence that each waits for the other to break.

She tugs at her skirt which hikes up her knees each time she moves. Why did she choose to wear this skirt today, when she seldom does? A faint sheen of embarrassment appears on her upper lip.

He notices it, and her hands as they tug at the hemline of her skirt. She has worn a short skirt to suggest what? Oh my Lee, he thinks, I would want you even if you were swathed in a tent. He rises from the chair and goes towards her and pulls her up from her chair. She looks at him. He looks at her. She smiles.

He bends his head and kisses her on the lips.

The warmth uncoils in the pit of her stomach. She leans into him. It's finally happening, she thinks.

'Stand on my feet,' he says softly. She does.

His hands move over her body, gently at first and then with a furious need as he gathers her into him. She sucks in her breath as she wraps her legs around his hips.

A little voice whispers in her head: is this for real? This is out of a movie!

His tongue probes her mouth open and then all thoughts stop except one: Whatever it is, this thing that has no name, I don't want to ever be out of it…is this love? Is this what they call love?

Over his shoulder she sees the fog growing denser. 'Ship,' she murmurs.

'What, baby?' he says.

She smiles against his shoulder. Baby? No one has called her baby in a long time.

'Ship, I think I'm falling in love with you,' she says, unable to help herself.

'You think?' he asks with a peculiar glint in his eye. 'And you are only just falling in love?'

She grins. 'I thought I would break it to you gently.'

He looks at the long table in the living room. A few scripts sit atop it and a stack of coasters. He walks towards it with her still wrapped around his hips. With one hand he sweeps everything off the table and then puts her down on it.

'And you?' she asks, wondering why she is doing so.

'I love you, Lee,' he murmurs. 'How can I not?'

He pushes her back on the table and again she thinks: Have I seen this in a movie? Have I seen him do precisely this?

'Don't, Lee,' he says, looming over her. 'Don't do that. I know what you are doing.'

'What?' she protests, wriggling as his breath fans the skin of her midriff where he has pulled up her T-shirt.

'This is for real. You and I. This is not from a movie. This is not in any script, Lee. This is me wanting to make love to you, my Lee.'

Her muscles unclench. She touches his cheek. 'Oh darling,' she says, running the back of her hand against the stubble on his scalp.

He removes her clothes and tosses them on a chair. She sits up to undress him. The T-shirt and track pants he wears are like a second skin. His body tenses under her touch.

She leans forward and takes his nipple in her mouth. He gasps in pleasure.

He pushes her back onto the table. 'Do you want to move to the bed?' he asks as his breath and lips trail a path from her mouth down her body.

'No,' she whimpers. The softness of the bed would cushion and absorb the feel of his body. On the table, she will feel him on her, within her.

Her back arches. A moan escapes her lips. He feeds on her as if she were the fount of miracles; he feeds on her as if she's the only sustenance he needs.

Her hips begin to move. He enters her with a hard thrust. There is a glitter in his eyes even as his lips pull back over his teeth.

The leopard growls. And she, his mate, meets him halfway, scouring his back with her nails, nipping his shoulder, yowling obscenities and endearments into his skin.

Abruptly he pauses. She clenches her hips around him. He licks the sweat off her face. 'What is this, Lee? What is this?' he demands through clenched teeth.

All that she was ceases to matter. All that she thinks she ought to be dies as their bodies move together. 'I don't know. I don't know where you end and where I begin,' she says as his fingers dig into her flesh.

Qollu – Leema's mother said the Madras gram, as she called it, was for horses. Suddenly everything fell into place. My aachi cooked qollu once every week. She put it into something or the other. A rasam or a poriyal, or she made chutney podi with it, which we ate with idlis, with a little oil mixed into it. I remember how my father wore a cloudy expression when she served it. 'I'm not enough for you, am I?' he demanded once. 'Shhh, the girl is listening,' she chided him. 'I just want you to keep your strength forever. That's all,' she smiled, caressing the side of his arm. I saw the secret smile on his lips and wondered what it was he needed his strength for. She did all the work in the house and helped him in the fields. If anyone needed to build her strength, I thought it was she.

QOLLU

Q

'How do you say qollu in English?' I ask her. It's half past twelve and she is sitting with a cup of coffee. She has just woken up and her eyelids are still heavy with sleep.

Leema yawns. 'Horsegram. Why?'

I shake my head. 'No, I mean, how would you write it?'

'Kollu or qollu…though I suppose Q is more appropriate. But why, Akka?'

She has an amused expression on her face. I feel my mouth tighten as she yawns languorously, this time stretching her arms above her head and arching her back. Like a cat, I think. A cat that has been petted and caressed and then fed a whole bowl of creamy milk. All it wants to do now is curl up in the sunshine and sleep. Till it's time for more caresses and cream.

I was that woman once. When my Rayar was in my life, we found a way to be with each other. If two people want it, they will find the time, hollow out the space and cradle into each other, no matter what. But both people must want it. During those months, I was the most fulfilled woman to walk the earth. He was the man I wanted him to be. And he said I was the woman he had hoped to meet someday in his life.

Foolish me. I thought that meant forever together. I thought we would move into the overseer's cottage perhaps. I saw us growing old together. I saw us feeding chickens in the backyard and harvesting our vegetables from the patch we planted together. I would watch him and think that I hadn't had enough of him. The years we were apart had been wasted. I was filled with a great sadness; the years left would never be enough.

Something in me snaps.

'I soaked some qollu for you,' I say. 'I'll make a sundal for you to eat at lunch.'

'It's horse fodder…you know I don't like it.'

A hardness creeps into me. 'Why do you think qollu is fed to the horses? To build their strength. You are going to need all the strength you have and more to keep fucking that actor.'

'What?' she whispers.

I am horrified at what I have said. But I cannot stop.

All the bitterness of the years past comes out like a torrent. She is the reason why my Rayar went away. 'You know you are like one of the mares they use to prepare the prize stallion before it ejaculates…just a teaser fuck. Do you think he is going to leave his wife for you? You can be sure that if he does, it will be for a champion mare waiting for his sperm. Someone with the right pedigree, who is the right age and the right everything!'

I stop. What am I saying? What am I doing? I see the horror on her face; it's more shock than anger. What have I done? I ask myself.

17

'I don't know what to think,' she says. He takes her hand in his as they walk.

'Don't tell me you are already running scared, Lee?' he says, caressing the side of her palm with a finger.

'No, not scared. But I can't get over what she said to me. The venom in her words and the fury in her eyes…' Lena says in a small voice.

He takes her in his arms. It's the middle of nowhere. All around are tea bushes. Slope after slope, and the tall wind-breaker trees with pepper vines. At any moment someone could emerge from the path between the tea bushes or turn the corner towards them.

She leans into him and wraps her arms around him. Despite the sting of Akka's words, an incredible sense of peace fills her. And joy. Just being with him makes her happy.

Has she been unhappy before? She doesn't know. But it has never been like this. That much she knows.

'She resents my presence…' Shoola Pani murmurs against her hair. 'She has never had to share you but now she feels her place in your life is threatened. So she is lashing out.'

'No, there's more to this than just feeling left out,' Lena says.

They resume walking. They don't hold hands but their arms touch as they walk.

He stops. She looks at him questioningly.

'Do you think that?' he asks.

'Do I think what?'

'That you are being used while my real life waits for me elsewhere.'

She drops her eyes. She has thought it ever since that first moment they mouthed the same words. It seemed a long time ago, even though it had been less than a week. Six days to be precise, she thinks.

'I do have a real life elsewhere but I am also in love with you,' he says.

The honesty of his admission moves her. She couldn't have taken it if he pretended otherwise and reassured her with lies.

The irony of an affair, she realizes, is that the only thing that can sanctify it is absolute honesty between two people. Only the truth can redeem it from being hollow words and the mere slaking of a physical need.

They enter the English cemetery. He picks two sprigs of honeysuckle growing on the hedge and threads them through her ear lobes. She smiles. 'Who do you think you are? Mellors?'

'Who?' he frowns.

'A character from a novel. The gamekeeper who threads flowers in Lady Chatterley's pubic hair.'

'Oh, him! I've seen the film,' he says as he adds more blossoms to her hair. 'And no, I didn't get the idea from the movie… Sometimes, Lee, you have to see me as a man. Just a man in love with a woman he can't keep his hands off. Will you?'

She sees him with an overwhelming sense of clarity; she has never met anyone like him and may never do so again. She nods. And as if to convince herself that he's for real, she touches the corner of his mouth with the tip of her finger.

Rava – Why is it that we don't respect this ingredient as we do arisi or godumai? To me rava is more versatile than the staples. During the rains, when little minnows appeared in the ditches that turned into rivers, the boys and I would catch them and put them into a Horlicks bottle. The boys wanted to feed them pori but I said that would be like a rat swallowing a cat. What do we feed them then, if not puffed rice? they demanded. That's when I thought of rava. The boys laughed, saying, our baby fish are eating upma now... I glared at them. The thing about food, be it grain or vegetable or meat or fish, is that one must know what one can serve to whom. Every ingredient has a purpose and a message.

RAVA

R

I stay awake all through the night, staring at the ceiling. It's probably the most miserable night of my life. Leema is my child. Almost. There aren't too many years between us, but I could have been her mother. I think of her as my child, the daughter I could have had. And it's this child I had lashed out at.

What can I say in my defense except that it has been long coming... For twenty-three years I have held it within me; a repressed rage at the unfairness of it all.

Leema was fourteen. I was thirty-three. And my Rayar was twenty-eight. Her mother thought it best that he be sent to work in the plains where they had a little hotel. She offered one of my own platitudes back to me: 'You don't keep a lit wick and cotton side by side, do you, Komathi?'

I didn't know what to say. How could I ask Rayar to stay back? Neither did he ask me to go with him.

Sometimes I wonder if I should have gone with him. But my son, whom I had left behind with my brother in Pollachi when I came to Valparai, was studying in a school there and if I went away, I feared his life would fall apart. On the other hand, if my life with Rayar worked out, I could send for my son and we could all live together. But what if it didn't? What if my Rayar and I fell out? Stolen embraces and secret kisses were all very well, but once we shared a roof and a bed, the rush of excitement alone wouldn't be enough to hold us together. I wouldn't have a job to come back to. My child would be branded the son of a slut… And so I did nothing but live a half-life built on memories and a deep sense of regret.

I don't know how I will face her again. I don't know how we are going to erase the words I spoke from both our minds.

Eventually I rise and go to the kitchen. I am not in the mood to cook anything complex. I decide to make upma. As I measure out the rava, I think of kesari and how much my Rayar detested it – as much as my Leema loved it. It was what caused the episode that took him away. I swore then that I would never cook it again for anyone and especially not for her.

He taught me to write his name. I trace the letter R on the kitchen table. Rayar. Rava. I have my R and I know what I must do.

I'll make rava kesari and when Leema comes for breakfast, I'll serve it to her. My kesari will say, forgive me, better than words can.

18

'My parents sent him away because of me. And Akka has had to live with that resentment simmering within her all these years. He was the love of her life. He was her everything and she lost him because of me,' Lena tells Shoola Pani.

Shoola Pani looks at her as she wrings her hands in consternation. The slender fingers seem even more fragile. 'You were a child, and your parents were only watching out for you.'

She moves to sit beside him. It seems like the safest place on the planet just now. Rather like the burrow she made for herself under the four-poster bed in her bedroom when she was a child. Akka was the only one who knew about it and she kept it dust-free and lint-clean. It was where she hid when her parents began their arguments.

First the scathing words, then the loud voices, the shouting and screaming, the dishes breaking, the slammed front door, the whimpering from the bedroom. Lena knew that if she hid in the burrow and spent the night there, praying to Mother Mary and Baby Jesus, all would be well again in the morning. Her parents would emerge from the bedroom smiling at each other.

He wraps his arms around her. She presses her cheek into the curve of his neck.

'We always assume children are innocent. Maybe it's what we want to believe. But I wasn't. I knew what I was doing. I was fourteen and a bit and there was Raghavendra, young and interesting-looking, with a cocky smile. A man. I thought I could wrap him around my little finger like Mummy had Papa around hers.'

'And he responded?' His voice is harsh.

'No, he saw me for the brat I was. Besides, I guess he was too much in love with Akka. I was her charge and that was all I was to him. To be humoured, so I didn't mess around too much with her. But I was silly. As silly as only a fourteen-year-old mixed-up girl can be.'

'And…' Shoola Pani doesn't want to think about what could have happened. 'What did he do to you?'

'It's more about what I did to him. I bullied him. I knew there was little he could do. He needed the job, I knew, and I wanted to see how far I could push him. Poor Raghavendra. He must have endured my pettiness and rudeness for Akka. He could have found another job easily enough, I know now.

'I think my mother noticed how I was always on his case. And then, one Sunday morning, Akka made kesari. Raghavendra detested it. He said it was too oily for his taste. I was eating it, sitting at the kitchen table, when he walked in. Akka was turning out the idlis. He made a face at me and said, "How can you eat that baby's vomit?"

'I remember narrowing my eyes. "Sit," I said to him. Akka stared in surprise. I felt heady with power. I was using the tone my mother brought out when she was admonishing the estate workers.

'Raghavendra looked uncertainly at Akka. She said, "Leema, what are you doing?"

'Raghavendra sat. Perhaps he was trying to prevent the moment from turning ugly. I went to stand near him. "Open your mouth," I said.

'He did. I spooned the kesari into his mouth. "Swallow!" I snapped. He did. I fed him the kesari spoon by spoon till the dish was almost empty. That was when my mother walked in and demanded, "What's going on?"

'Akka was trying to protect me when she said, "Leema was giving him a taste of the kesari. That's all, madam."

'Perhaps if she had spoken the truth and said I was bullying him, nothing would have changed.

'But Mummy interpreted it as something else. He was sent away. I never thought about it. Once he left, I forgot about him. And all these years she has thought about nothing else. Him and the dreams they dreamt together.'

He feels the wetness of her tears against his skin. Why had Komathi not gone to her Raghavendra either? Pride, or fear? How callously we treat what we should treasure, he thinks with a pang. 'Lee,' he murmurs, 'Lee, darling. Don't.'

Sora – Since we lived some distance from the sea, we didn't get as much fish as we would have liked. It was mostly river fish and karuvaad. But just after my aachi had my youngest brother, my father brought home sora. It was supposed to be good for mothers who were breast feeding. But my aachi didn't like it very much. I think I ate it all. I thought I wouldn't mind having half a dozen children just to be able to eat it. Then we saw a film at the cinema kottai. It was called Juice or Jaws or something like that. I can't remember. It was set in a faraway country and was about a giant sora that attacked people in the sea, ripping their legs off and leaving a trail of blood. How could something so vicious taste so good? I thought, wondering how many bits of human flesh the sora I ate had chewed. I never ate sora again.

SORA

S

KK is back. As always, he has returned with something that isn't available in the hills. Sora. A whole fish with head, tail, fins and a list of dishes I must make with it.

Leema's face is drawn. What is she going to do? How is she going to juggle her feelings without hurting either man or herself in the process?

She comes to stand by my side as I place the fish on the washing stone. I have the cleaver in my hand.

'Akka,' she says.

I look at her. She moves the body of the fish this way and that.

'What is it, Leema?' I ask. I know what is coming. She will ask me to speak a few untruths to mask her doings while KK was away. I also know I will lie for her, even knowing that I will be sent to hell where my flesh will be branded and my teeth pulled out one by one. They say that in hell the skin and teeth will grow back by morning so the demons can continue with their torture day after day. That is hell. No respite from anguish. No hope that something will change and life will get better.

'How can I ask you to forgive me?' she says. 'I took away your chance of happiness.'

'You didn't,' I tell her quietly.

'Well, I was responsible for what happened.'

I close my eyes for a moment. 'Don't,' I say. 'Don't beat yourself up about it. Rayar didn't come looking for me. He could have. And even if we had lived together, who knows how it would have turned out?

'And that's the truth. I don't know. Perhaps we would have ended up hating each other.'

I look at the fish lying on the stone. It resembles the letter of an alphabet. 'What is this letter?' I ask.

'Could be an S,' she says with a small smile.

'Yes, the sora is perfect for an S. It is a sound and a letter. A sora is neither an animal nor a fish, is it?'

'I don't know if that's true, Akka,' she says.

'It lives in the water and looks like a fish, but it tastes like meat.'

She gives me a strange look as she leaves me to skin and chop the sora. With the head I will make a curry. With the meat fillets, I will make a sora fry. To the bits and pieces I tease out of the skin I will add some shredded dam fish, and that is what I will use to make sora puttu. The seasoning and the strong flavour of the sora will camouflage the muddy taste of the freshwater fish from the dam.

It's a compromise, but life is all about compromises and when Leema has eaten the sora puttu, I will tell her about the true value of compromise in our lives.

19

When Lena knocks on his door, she hears music playing from within. It sounds almost like a chanting, resonant of mountains and vast empty spaces.

He opens the door, smiles, takes her hand in his and leads her to the sofa. Without letting go of her hand, he sits and pulls her down by his side. She rests her head against his arm. She closes her eyes and tunes everything out except the beating of his heart and the pure notes of the woman singing in a language she has never heard before. She knows every inch of his body, but for the first time she is conscious of him at another level: the curve of his foot, the strong blue veins that snake up his arms, the rasp of his stubble, the strength of his thighs, the shadow of a scar on his cheek, the smell of his skin…

When the singing stops, she feels as though she has walked through a bamboo grove alongside a tinkling stream under a clear blue sky. 'Who is she?'

'Ani Choying Drolma; they call her the singing nun,' he says. 'Lee, when I listen to her, I imagine myself in a bamboo grove alongside a river and the sky is clear and blue, as it can be only high up in the mountains.'

She sighs. 'Ship, that's exactly what I was thinking.'

His arms tighten around her.

'He's back,' she says.

'And?'

'And I don't know.'

'What are we going to do?'

'I don't know,' she says. 'I don't want to be unfair to KK or to your family. I know you have one, even if you have never mentioned them. I don't want to be the reason for you to jeopardize your movie career or diminish your standing with your fans. But I don't know how I'm going to cope without you in my life. And I don't know if I can be this bit on the side either.'

She gets up and walks to the window.

'I thought I was escaping complications when I came here.' She hears the wry note in his voice, but chooses not to acknowledge it.

Instead, she gives into her secret fear as she demands, 'Do you want me to walk away and never look back?'

'Lee,' he says. 'You know you can't do that and I won't let you either. I didn't think through what was happening between us. The pace at which it happened didn't let me. Did you, Lee?' He goes to stand by her and then leads her to the inner room.

'I didn't,' she says. 'I just went with the flow.'

'Flow?' He laughs against her mouth. 'It was the rapids and we were white-water rafting.'

She laughs and he catches her lower lip between his teeth in a gentle nibble. 'Don't think so much, Lee…we'll figure it out.'

How can she think of anything anyway, while his hands are moving over her body and his breath is fanning her skin. He doesn't make love with the tenderness she expects from him but with a barely reined-in brutality. Pushing her against the wall of the room, he licks the line of her jaw. She sees his eyes; there is an animal glint in them.

His teeth graze her skin. His hands push up her skirt and bunch it around her waist. She snaps open the buttons on his shirt and lets her fingers splay on his chest.

He growls as he squats on his haunches and yanks down her panties in one swift move. 'Why do you wear these things?' he asks, dangling the scrap of purple lace from his fingers.

She laughs and draws in her breath as his tongue seeks her out, making her thrust against his face. Then it is she who pushes his head away and pulls him up so she can go down on him. He sucks in his breath loudly as she takes him in her mouth.

All the uncertainties, the fears, the not knowing dissipate when he enters her. She shudders as he thrusts into her again and again murmuring, 'Lee, my Lee…'

'Don't close your eyes,' he says. I need to see you and know what's happening to you.'

And then it becomes impossible to hold back and as he explodes inside her, she bites down on his shoulder. They hold each other and there it is again: the sensation of walking through the bamboo grove alongside a stream. He murmurs, 'I hear it, Lee, I hear it. You and I by that stream under the cold blue sky. Just you and I in our private world.'

With a swift change in mood, he slaps her buttocks playfully and says, 'I was thinking of something this morning.'

She stares at his face, wondering at the stranger in front of her.

Thayir – How was milk first set to turn into a wobbly mass you could slice through? Who first thought of putting it into their mouth? One thing is certain: then, as now, thayir slides down your throat, leaving a trail of cool wetness that heals your insides as much as your frazzled nerves. Is that why they feed elephants in masth hot rice into which thayir has been stirred, I wonder. In the days after my Rayar left, I used to eat steaming hot rice into which I had stirred thayir. It numbed my senses and caused my eyes to droop and I slept the sleep of the dead, wishing I would never have to wake up again.

THAYIR

T

KK is unwell. He usually is after being away from home. I don't know if it's a weak stomach or excessive eating while he is away. I can hear Leema admonish him. 'Why do you eat at those little road-side restaurants? It's for people with cast-iron insides who work the grease off with the work they do.'

He groans. My Leema may be many things, but she is a hopeless nurse. Her bedside manner is that of a school headmistress scolding a naughty child. And since her actor seems to have gone away, she has been in a foul mood. It's best that she stay away from KK, I think, so I shoo her out and tell her to go to the crèche.

I make kashayam with jeera, dried inji and omam. It will settle his stomach. He takes it from me with a grateful smile.

'Will you make some moru kaachiyathu?' he asks.

I nod. Nearly once every ten days I seem to make it for him. His mother showed me how to do it.

'He's going to need it,' she had laughed. She had a hearty laugh, and an equally hearty appetite and zest for life. It occurred to me that her boisterousness had turned him into the cold, reticent creature he was. Like a turtle withdrawing into its shell, he had found refuge in silence. But she knew her son better than anyone else, even though they had spent very little time together. Him in boarding school and they elsewhere.

'You can be sure that he will not say one nice word about your cooking even if he stuffs his face silly. And if he does, you won't know if he is paying you a compliment or being sarcastic. So please don't be upset,' she said in an apologetic tone.

'And this moru kaachiyathu, you will need to make it for him when he has one of his stomach upsets.'

She died a couple of years ago but her kashyamam and moru kaachiyathu lives on.

'Why does he have these frequent stomach upsets?' I asked her once.

She shrugged. 'Greed. He doesn't know how to control himself when he sees things he likes to eat. And then the guilt sits in his belly along with the oil, meat and everything else. Just like it was with father.' She laughed loudly, but I heard the rueful note and wondered what demons she was seeking to exorcise with her bonhomie.

I whip the thayir in the mixie with some water to make moru. Without curd it is impossible to serve a meal. It goes into the pachadi and kozhambu, it goes into marinades and to tenderize meat.

It isn't easy to set perfect wobbly thayir. The temperature of the milk, the vessel we use to set it in, the few drops of curd needed to start the batch, everything is crucial. And then it has to be left alone.

A little like an affair of the heart. Sometimes people need to take a conscious break from each other. Just to see how set you are with each other and on your own. For if you are not happy on your own, how can you be happy with another person?

20

Lena sits with the children at the crèche. Their eager faces and incessant patter fill some of the hollowness within her. Two nights ago, she had received his text:

Have to go to Pollachi. Will be back first thing day after.

She wonders what could be so important that Biju couldn't handle it on his own. Shadows dance. Flickering doubt, suspicion and jealousy. The young film-maker had said she was scouting for locations in the region. Did he have a special name for her as well?

It's already two days and she hasn't heard from him yet. She takes the road from the mattom square to Hikes division. Her feet drag. The dense clouds that cover the sun are a mere extension of the grey within her.

She looks for signs that will tell her that the day is going to get better: a sun beam she can walk towards, a crow pheasant that would rise from a tree, a purple flower…

In a gutter behind a culvert, she hears a whining. She steps across the road and finds a little puppy amidst the stones. Has someone left it there knowing it won't survive? Everyone here knows leopards love dog meat and the puppy will be taken by a cat on the prowl soon.

It's a deep gutter and she wonders how she can reach the puppy without breaking a leg or twisting an ankle. Then she hears the sound of an SUV. She turns around and her heart soars.

It is him.

He pulls alongside and steps out. She hurls herself into his arms.

He looks at her surprised. 'I guess you missed me, Lee,' he says with a laugh.

She smiles and smiles, unable to stop.

'What are you doing here? I went looking for you in the crèche and the ayah said she saw you head this way. She sounded concerned and rather disapproving. What's with this division?' His gaze sweeps the lonely slopes of tea.

She flushes. 'It's not considered safe.'

'You're the boss. Who's going to attack you?'

'The elephants and leopards don't know I'm the boss.' She laughs, seeing his eyes dart around, up and down.

'And you came here on your own?' he asks, frowning.

'It's the only road we haven't taken. There's nothing here to remind me of you?' She looks away so he doesn't see her lip wobble.

He squeezes her hand. 'Oh Lee,' he murmurs.

'I need your help,' she says, leading him towards the gutter.

He sees the whimpering puppy. 'Oh no!' He shakes his head. 'What do you want me to do?'

'Get down there and bring the puppy up.'

'Me?' He looks startled.

'Hey, you are the hero.' She frowns. 'Don't you do this in all your movies?'

'That's the movies, Lee, and I have stuntmen who do all the risky stuff. I'm just tinsel, make-up and special effects…'

'In which case I'll go down and you can go fetch help if I can't haul myself up,' she says, edging her way to the deep gutter.

'No, I'll do it,' he says.

She hides a smile. Men, movie stars or mechanics, are the same.

She watches him as he drops into the gutter and picks up the puppy. He hands it over to her and hauls himself up in one fluid motion. He is truly like a leopard, she thinks.

'Thank you,' she mouths as she holds the puppy to her bosom.

The puppy whimpers and she cuddles it.

'Do you baby-talk everything?' he asks, looking at her as he starts the vehicle.

'Everything,' she says, holding his gaze.

'I can't take him home,' she says. 'The dogs are fiercely jealous and will need to be introduced to him slowly.'

'What will you do?' he asks.

'Keep him in the crèche for a while maybe. But he's so little and I don't like the thought of him being alone at night.' She watches the fat little puppy slip out of her hands, clamber across the seat and plant himself in Ship's lap.

'Unless…' she begins softly.

He looks at the puppy sitting on his lap. 'Oh well,' he sighs.

It feels strange to have an animal in his lap. He has never thought of himself as an animal person. But neither is he who he is supposed to be when with Lee.

Uzunthu – This one is truly the prince among parpu. It adds taste to a dish, is good for health, and can leaven a batter unlike other parpus. There would be no idli or dosai if there was no uzunthu. Sometimes I think uzunthu is a lot like hope. When the days stretch pointlessly ahead, the only thing that can give it some meaning is hope rising to the surface. But I have also heard that too much of uzunthu causes deafness. I am not surprised. One needs to even hope in moderation. Otherwise, like an appalam into which too much uzunthu has gone, it will puff out and shatter into shards.

UZUNTHU

U

As I take out half a cup of white uzunthu to soak, I wonder if uzunthu begins with the letter U.

Leema comes in with the expression of a child who has seen a rainbow. 'Akka,' she says. 'I think you should sit down. I have some news for you.'

'What?' I ask as she hurries me into a chair. 'But first tell me, would uzunthu be right for U?'

'Are you still on that?' she laughs. 'Forget the alphabet for a moment. Listen to me…guess what Shoola Pani did?'

I shake my head. What can he have done? I have no idea. 'Tell me, would uzunthu be right for U?'

'Yes, yes,' she says impatiently. 'Don't you want to hear my news?

'He went looking for your Rayar.'

My heart stills. I close my eyes. 'And he found him?' I drop my head in my hands.

'He has built a house in Pollachi,' Leema says, unable to hide her excitement. 'Shoola Pani said it's a lovely little house.'

I look up at her. 'It has roses in the front and jasmine bushes. It has marikolanthu and kanakambaram flowers. There are vegetables growing in the backyard and chickens squawking and scratching in the dirt.'

'How do you know?' she asks and then touches my arm gently. 'You have seen it.'

I shake my head. 'No, but we talked about it.'

And then I ask, unable to prevent the bitterness coating my tongue from seeping into my words, 'Did your actor also see Rayar's wife?'

'He doesn't have a wife, Akka,' she says.

'I heard that he married.'

'He did once. But he lives alone now.'

I feel as though someone has clubbed me on the head.

'Maybe we can go visit him.' The words hang in the air.

I walk out of the room. I do not know what to think. All these years, hope kept me going. That one day my Rayar would seek me out.

He lives in Pollachi. He has built a home that we dreamt about. He married. But now he is alone. Yet he never came for me. Perhaps I read too much into what was a mere matter for him. That's how men refer to sex. Matter.

Uzunthu parpu needs to be measured out with a careful hand. Too little and the batter becomes stodgy and turns out idlis like rock and vadas like rubber wheels. Too much can cause the batter to rise so high that it takes away its substance.

Hope is a lot like that. I should have measured my dreams out with the same careful hand.

21

'She was devastated, Ship.'

Shoola Pani looks up from the puppy he is fondling.

'I didn't think of you as a dog person,' she smiles.

'Neither did I.' This is a man who has walked into a situation he wasn't prepared for but loves it so much that he is loath to extricate himself from it.

'Did you tell her he is single?' he asks.

She nods.

'And?'

'She walked out of the kitchen and stood with her back to me.'

The puppy leaps out of his lap. 'Perhaps I should tell her what I saw. And what he said to me.'

'Would you?'

He holds out his hand to her. 'Of course!'

As they walk towards the bungalow, Lena sees that KK is at his habitual place at the roll-top desk at the end of the parlour. 'He is home,' she says.

'Does it matter?' he asks softly.

'I don't know.'

'I'll just say hello and go talk to Komathi.'

Shoola Pani steps forward and offers his hand to

KK. 'Hello,' he says. 'I need to ask your cook about a recipe.'

KK nods and watches bemused as Lena directs the actor towards the kitchen.

'Oh now, the actor has turned chef, has he?' KK murmurs when she comes back and sits down. KK, she notices, is glancing at his watch every few minutes. Finally, he asks, 'What's going on, Lena?'

Her heart stills. 'What do you mean?' she frowns.

'How long is he going to be here? We are organizing a camp for the tribals. The medical officer from Parry Agro wanted me to pitch in. I really need to leave.'

'The Kadas?' she asks.

He nods. 'Why didn't you tell me? We would have come too,' she says. Ship would have loved it.

'It's not a movie set. It's the real jungle. He would be a nuisance.' KK's mouth twists as he starts packing his rucksack.

'Aren't you generalizing?' she snaps.

'And aren't you hovering around him a little too much?' KK demands in turn. 'You don't want him thinking you are a star-struck groupie, do you?'

She laughs delicately. 'I don't think you need to worry about that. I think he likes my company because I am not star-struck.'

Then, unable to resist, she asks, 'Are you jealous?'

His eyebrows rise. 'Me! Why would I be? Besides, if the tabloids are right, you are a little too old for his liking. Movie stars like nymphets.'

She looks away so he doesn't see the bleakness in her eyes. It's as if he has struck at the very heart of her uncertainty.

She rises from her chair. 'Carry on with your day, KK…let me find out what's going on in the kitchen.'

KK leaves shaking his head, as if the very thought of his dependable Lena having an affair with an ageing movie star is one of the drollest things anyone could suggest.

She sees Ship by the door. How much has he heard?

Varak – I didn't even know the gilt on sweets had a name until my Rayar said so. So who makes the varak? I asked. The goldsmith or the cook? In any case, why would anyone want to gild a sweet? And for what jóy?

VARAK

V

Once my Rayar brought a box of peda for me from Bombay. There were sixteen of them, stacked four on top of each other. On top of each peda was a gold sheet. I had never seen anything like it before. The silver on sweets and even on a peda I was familiar with, but gold was something else.

'You know what they call this?' he asked.

I shook my head, unable to take my eyes off the gold on the peda. I didn't have a single gram of gold to call my own and here were sweets wearing gold as an adornment.

'Varak,' he smiled. 'It's a Samskrutham word.'

'I have seen silver, but gold…never,' I said.

He took a peda from the box and bit into it. Then he offered it to me. I reached for it but he shoved my hand away and brought it to my lips. I opened my mouth and he slid it in. The peda tasted not of milk or sugar or gold, or whatever gold must taste like, but of him. His mouth.

He smiled slowly and asked, 'Do you like it?'

I flushed, unable to meet his gaze.

'The gold varak is used as an aphrodisiac,' he murmured. 'Though I don't think I'll ever need anything like that when I'm with you.'

I felt like a queen. I felt like Parvathi, powerful and potent. I felt like a woman does when she is loved for her body as much as for who she is.

That evening we spoke of our dreams. The house we would have and the life we would lead. It was these he took and made with someone else. It is this I cannot forgive him for. Not that he married and made a life. But that he usurped what he and I dreamt together.

The varak, be it gold or silver, is tasteless. It is mere adornment, but without it a peda is just a block of solidified sweetened milk. Our dreams are what make us who we are.

With a knife, I drew a V on the table. V for Varak. V for the deep scores in me.

I told the actor this when he tried to persuade me to go with him and Leema to Rayar's house.

He looked at me for a long moment and then quietly walked away.

22

He looks at his phone, scrolling down, reading the text messages. Those first few days, they had texted each other throughout the day. Courtship in fifth gear, he thinks.

Ship: *Wakey wakey*

Lee: *Have bn awake since 4.45*

Ship: *Whaaat? Morning person? Or sleeping disorder?*

Lee: *Morning person…sing to t birds & bees…need time for that*

Ship: *Ah luxuries only a plantation lady can afford. Lucky ya*

Lee: *What luxuries? I steal t time*

Ship: *That's a skill. U should write a book on how to do that*

Ill buy it & give it to all my movie buddies.

Art of stealing time! by Lena Memsahib

Lee: *You heard that, did you?*

Ship: :-) *I did… I did! Memsahib*

Lee: *What weather huh?*

Ship: *Lovelyyy*

Lee: *I love the rain*

Ship: *Hey, guess what? I tried scrolling up to review our messages to figure out when we clicked. I gave up*

Lee: *U mean when we actually started talking*

Or messaging?

Ship: *Actually talking*

Lee: *After our second meeting, rgt?*

Ship: *A strange & sudden sense of familiarity*

Lee: *Yes, that was how it was for me too. Hey, r we meeting tomorrow morning. I'd like to see u if possible*

Ship: *U r unbelievably sweet. Who knew?*

Lee: *Is that t impression I give? Of being un-sweet? :-)*

Ship: *No I didn't mean that. I never knew we would get so close*

Thick as thieves

Lee: *Yes…it happened so quickly*

Ship: *We should try n decode it together. Or do we need to decode at all??*

Lee: :-)

Ship: *Where r u sitting? what r u doing?*

Lee: *I watch this TV series called t good wife*:-)

So every week day fm 9 pm

Ship: *Ouch, what a title, lol*

Lee: *I know*:-)

The dance of the butterflies as they hover around each other, antennae quivering.

The joyful insouciance of those first forty-eight hours had been replaced by a clawing neediness to touch and touch and never let go. When their bodies meshed, it seemed they had moved to another plane. But his time here is drawing to an end. It was all very well for him to tell Biju that he didn't know when he was coming back. But the truth is, he will have to return soon.

It may not be to the life he once had. It may be a transformed version of that life. Or, who knows, it may be back to what he knows. The lure of the familiar and the comfort it offers are not to be sneered at. But what about Lee? What about them?

Lena is at the crèche. Outside, in the sandpit, Dulari is pouring sand from one cup to the other. She thinks of the text conversation Ship and she had that morning.

Lee: *Heard about Robin Williams?*

Ship: *Yeah…first thing in t morning…*

Its t fate of most creative people. Alcohol, drugs or suicide. U better plan a wreath for me:-)

Lee: *I wonder y. I don't think its loneliness*

What do ya think

N y do u think about suicide??

Ship: *There is sm loneliness. There is t constant battle with self-doubt. There is a darkness that weighs heavily*

It's part of every creative person's make up & t more successful u get t more it haunts…

Self-doubt and darkness are connected at least for me

I have a huge heavy dark side…that drags me to an abyss

Its hard work keeping it at bay…

An actor killing himself in Hollywood. Why would it impact her so much, except that Ship is an actor too. And there is no escaping the knowledge that what they have is as fragile as a narrow wire stretching between them. She has her life. This. He has his life. Elsewhere. Stay with me: someone has to say it first.

Who will it be? Him or her? Who will dare step off that tightrope first?

Wendiyum – Fenugreek: that's what it is called in English. I learnt its name from a foreigner who once came to stay with us. She was Leema's friend from college when Leema was in London. She hovered in the kitchen all day, wanting to know what was what, what went into what... She was most curious about wendiyum because she hadn't seen it before. I dissuaded her from using it in the dishes she cooked, occasionally adding our masalas to whatever mess she was creating. The wendiyum isn't a malleable spice. When you roast it one shade browner than it should be, it loses its flavour and becomes acrid and bitter. Add an extra pinch of wendiyum powder to a fish curry and it can ruin the flavour of the fish... Like advice, I think.

One should know when to and when not to. One should know how much would be just right and when to shut up.

WENDIYUM

W

Leema comes to me in the evening. Her face is drawn and there are shadows beneath her eyes. My little girl is finally a woman.

It isn't a child in your womb or even the mere presence of a womb that makes you a woman, I told her that when they brought her home after the pregnancy went wrong. They had removed her womb. It was the only time I saw her distraught.

'What will make me a woman then?' she asked.

'You will know when it happens to you,' I told her. I saw the scepticism in her eyes. I was an illiterate woman who had done nothing with her life. What would I know?

'You could adopt a child,' I said.

She nodded half-heartedly. 'Yes, we could.'

But they never did. KK had his dogs. I wonder if

he would have loved his children as much. And she had the crèche and an endless line of babies who came and went. I saw the loneliness in her eyes become part of her until she didn't know any better. Then, in the past few days I saw it explode and lift away like a cotton ball bursting open.

'Are you unwell?' I ask. Are you all right, I mean.

'A little tired,' she says. I don't know what she means.

And then suddenly she turns to me and rests her forehead on my shoulder. 'What am I going to do, Akka?'

I pat her head and sit her down. I think of the evening after I aborted Rayar's child. I sat like this, unable to decide if I wanted to live or die. And Leema's grandmother, who saw much but said little, made me a dish they called uluvachoru in their village. An old-fashioned dish hardly anyone makes any more, she said, but one that is good to build strength.

It was a rice dish made of wendiyum. A spice I knew well enough, but I had never eaten a dish that was made of just wendiyum.

I turn to her. 'Wendiyum? Can I spell it with a W?'

She stares at me uncomprehendingly and then bursts into laughter. I can hear the hysterical edge to that laughter and I feel as if my heart is breaking.

23

Lena paces up and down the corridor. She feels the gaze of several people following her. Akka and KK. Rosie, the top worker, and even the dogs watch her relentless pacing. But she is unable to sit down or lie on the bed. As long as she is walking, she feels as if she is in control. The truth is, she doesn't feel in control of anything – her emotions, her life, her being.

Komathi asks her, 'What's wrong?'

'Life.'

'You have a good life,' Akka says.

Lena looks at her. 'It isn't a bad life, but it's an empty one.' Lena is tired of saying all the things people want to hear.

Lena drums the kitchen table with her fingers. She waits for the older woman to say something. But she stands still and silent.

'I am a wife. I have a life here.'

'What do you want to do?'

'The thing is, it all happened so quickly that I never thought of what next.'

'And now?' Komathi asks, washing the few dishes in the sink.

'And now I realize that he will leave soon and I don't know what I'll do once he is gone.' Lena's voice cracks.

'Will you go with him if he asks you to?' Komathi asks, looking up from the dishes.

Lena stares. Will he? She hasn't even considered the possibility. Here, amidst the tea slopes and shola, their relationship has grown and blossomed into a magical marvellous thing. But away from it, would it survive? Reality has a curious way of peeling away the magic until all that is left is the nothingness of a crumbled dream.

'Your wendiyum rice doesn't seem to have helped,' Lena murmurs almost facetiously.

'If a dish could make a woman strong enough to ignore the call of her heart, then the world would be ruled by women. There would be no tears or shattered dreams…there would be no wars or bloodshed.' Komathi snorts, wiping her hands on a towel strung by the sink.

'You have to be strong,' she says. 'No matter what you decide, you have to be strong for yourself.'

*

Shoola Pani looks at his phone. There are countless messages and missed calls. The puppy whines.

'I have to go back. It's been twenty-three days since I got here,' he tells the puppy.

It cocks its head and looks at him, wagging its tail.

Shoola Pani smiles and squats on the ground to scratch behind the puppy's ear. 'I envy you,' he tells the puppy. 'You ask for what you want and you don't worry about the consequences. Do you?'

The puppy turns its head and licks his fingers as if to say: you must try it sometime. Unless you ask, how will you know?

There is nothing I can think of for the letter X. Then I remember the 'X' mark they put on poison bottles, transformer cages and danger zones. That is when I know that X is to tell myself to be cautious. To never forget that mistakes can be made. No matter how many times I have cooked a dish, I cannot let it leave the kitchen till I have tasted it.

X

Sometimes you can get all the ingredients right, you can measure them out exactly as you have been taught, you can chop and grind, sauté and simmer, use the right vessel on the desired heat, watch the dish so it doesn't boil over or burn and then you serve it in the nicest bowl available. And no one says a word as they taste it but you see how they don't touch it and shove it aside.

'What's wrong?' you demand.

One says: too much spice.

Another says: I think the vegetable isn't cooked enough.

And yet another says: it isn't how it tastes when you usually make it...maybe there were weevils in the parpu.

That's when you realize that you have made the

fatal mistake. You didn't taste it. You thought you had done everything right, so how could it go wrong?

That is what I must tell Leema. Be it a dish or life itself, one needs to taste it as one goes along. This is a mistake both a novice and an experienced cook can make. For recipe books and learning will never teach you the importance of instinct and taste. It is the X of my alphabet book. The danger signal of complacency or laziness.

It's not about doing too little or doing too much. It's about wresting control of your own life. It's what I failed to do. And if I don't tell Leema, she won't either.

Instead she will do what most of us women veer towards. Cook timidly. Live timidly. Letting everyone else tell us how we must cook, how we must live.

And all because we forget that we must make our lives to suit our taste, and not someone else's.

24

He wears a pensive look when they walk towards the cemetery. She wonders what he is thinking about. But it is he who asks her, 'What are you thinking?'

The puppy is on a leash. Lena is nervous about taking him out. One of the estate workers had spotted a leopard two evenings ago. But he is in a strange mood, unwilling to listen to reason.

'Are you happy, Ship?' she asks.

He looks at her blankly and says, 'I have to return.'

She looks away so he won't see her eyes fill.

'I dread going back,' he says.

She takes a deep breath. 'I dread your going away.'

He gives her a sidelong glance.

'Each morning when I wake up, I wonder if this will be the day you say you are leaving. But I didn't dare mention how I feel,' she says.

'Why?' He frowns, tugging the puppy away from a hole in the ground it seems determined to disappear into.

'I didn't want to scare you. I didn't want to weigh down our time together with expectations.'

They walk into the English cemetery. Their Arcadia.

They sit on the grave of the fallen angel. The puppy sniffs around and collapses into a heap on a patch of grass. They look at the puppy.

'He doesn't have a name,' he says.

'The children at the crèche will name him,' she says, reaching out to tug the puppy's ears.

'I was thinking of keeping him,' he says.

She looks at him in surprise. 'He's a mongrel and will probably grow into an ugly-looking dog. Not the kind of pure-bred looks that movie stars' dogs have.' The bitterness in her voice startles him.

He takes her hand in his. 'Don't generalize, Lee. You know I don't care about such things.'

The cemetery is loud with silence. Even the whistling schoolboy bird, who is otherwise everywhere, is absent.

'I don't know. That's the problem, you see. I know nothing about you. What is your favourite colour? The side of the bed you like to sleep on, and whether you snore. When you brush your teeth, do you go from left to right or the other way? Do you have a memory that makes you cringe? A memory that makes you cry? Do you like caramel popcorn? I know so little about you, Ship and...' She stops, unable to continue.

He puts an arm around her and nuzzles her cheek. 'I don't have a favourite colour. I like to sleep on the right side of the bed. I snore, but if you prod me, I'll stop. I don't know how I brush my teeth. Do you? I just brush. I like caramel popcorn. As for bad memories, what is past is past... I don't like to think about it.'

So that's it. When he leaves, this sojourn too will go into that category of 'past is past', not to be dwelt upon.

'Will you go with me?' he asks.

'What?' she asks.

'I asked if you will go with me, Lee?'

'You do realize I am married,' she whispers.

'Yes, so am I.' His mouth twists into a parody of a smile. 'What do you want, Lee?' he asks.

She wraps her arms around her knees and buries her head between them. 'I didn't think you would ask me to go with you.'

He looks away to get a grip on his feelings. When he was a young boy, his friends and he had gone to Marina beach one Sunday. The beach was the lure but there were also the freak shows: the three-headed baby, the woman with four arms... As a movie star, he has seen the same eagerness and almost morbid curiosity in the eyes of the crowds that gather around him. In the end, that's all it comes down to. He's just another attraction in a freak show.

'I guess I have my answer. You thought I would leave and…this would be over? Is that what it is? Something in your bucket list: fuck a movie star.' His voice is low but the fury in it makes her wince.

'Ship,' she says and puts her hand on his arm.

He gets up. 'Let's go,' he tells the puppy, tugging at the leash.

The puppy springs up. They walk to the gate. He turns to look at her. 'Are you coming?'

She shakes her head and looks away. Does he realize what he is asking of her?

He stands there. She can feel him watching her. Then a strange blankness.

When she looks again, he is gone. She wonders if her hesitation has hurt him. Or is he just not used to rejection of any sort?

Yera – Many years ago, when I was cleaning yera, Leema asked me what I was thinking of. 'You have such a strange expression on your face,' she said. I looked at her unseeingly. What had I been thinking of? I didn't know. 'Whenever I clean yera, my mind goes on a trip without telling me where it went,' I said.

'It's called prawn,' Leema said. In those days she was teaching me the English word for everything. Porn, I repeated. She giggled and left the room. What did I say? I wondered.

YERA

Y

Muthu's face is like a sunflower in bloom. His friend the bus driver has brought him a bag of yera. 'Sir asked me to order some,' he says, afraid I will scold him. Cleaning yera is tedious, and after all that back-breaking work, you get just a handful to cook.

I empty the bag of yera into a colander. An antenna stabs me. I flinch. The yera's antennae can be vicious and extremely painful.

Lena peers into the colander. 'Here is your Y, Akka. Y for Yera. Are you going to clean it now?'

I nod. Yera has a way of stinking up the house and, god knows what there is about it, but it brings a swarm of houseflies almost immediately.

I twist the head off one. Then I snap open the shell with my fingers. With a knife I split the back of the yera and pull out the black vein.

I saw Leema's face when she came home yesterday. She may as well have died.

I dangle the black vein in her face. 'This is like regret,' I say. 'If you give it room, it will take over your life and poison your tomorrows.'

25

A little after lunch, Lena lies in bed replaying in her mind every moment from the time she went to greet the guest at Mimosa Cottage twenty-five days ago. That first meeting could have gone three ways: she could have walked away, offended by his rudeness; he needn't have apologized or invited her in. Instead he had and, despite his surliness, she had stayed on and their lives had changed.

There had been a 33.333 per cent chance that their lives would collide and find a new trajectory of its own. When you total up 33.333 three times, you get 99.999. What is that .001 particle that steers chance in one direction? From her random amalgamation of trivia, a phrase floats into her thoughts: the god particle. The mysterious force that gives mass to matter. The mysterious god particle had ensured that their destinies would collide and connect.

But there is no corollary to the consequences of heeding the god particle, Lena thinks with a rueful smile. She turns on her side and buries her face in the pillow.

It's a little past 4 p.m. when Lena wakes up from

her siesta. She had slept heavily and deeply. She goes to the dining room and sees a note Muthu has left on the table. It's from Ship. She reads it, then goes back in and grabs a shawl to wrap around herself. The dogs look at her as she walks past them. She stops and whispers in their ears. Ringo licks her hand. Star drops his head on his paws.

She walks down the steps towards the cottage. Ship is by his SUV and the puppy is on a leash. They haven't met or spoken in the last twenty-four hours. She sees that he is throwing a bag into the vehicle.

She walks towards him. 'I have a name for him,' she says.

He looks at her.

'But I'll tell you the name only when we get there.'

A smile starts on his face and ends on hers.

He opens the door on the passenger side for her. She gets in. He hands the puppy to her.

He gets in and reverses. He still hasn't spoken.

He puts on the Singing Nun's song. Then he turns to her and asks, 'Are you happy, Lee?'

'Are you happy, Ship?' she retorts.

He takes her hand and places it beneath his on the gear stick. And then, with his fingers entwined with hers, he changes the gear.

Zigarthanda – There is no English name for this drink. There is nothing like it available anywhere else in the world, I am certain. All I can say is that it is a tall, cold drink made of milk into which the gum of the badam tree is added. Is that why it makes you feel that you can deal with anything in life? An old love. A new love. The limbo in between. The waiting. The wanting. The not knowing what might become of your tomorrows.

———————————————

ZIGARTHANDA

Z

Once, just once, my Rayar and I went away for three days to Madurai. He took me to a little place where he bought me a local specialty, Zigarthanda.

'What is it?' I asked suspiciously.

'Try it,' my Rayar smiled.

'But it looks like milk.'

'So?'

'I don't drink milk. Was never given any when I was a child, so I can't bear the taste of it,' I said.

'This isn't milk as you know it,' my Rayar said, thrusting the glass towards me.

The dimple in his cheek dipped and I thought I would drink it for him even if it tasted like cat's pee.

I think of how the Zigarthanda slid down my throat. This must be amrutham, I thought. It was cool and sweet, refreshing and full of flavour. What comes hereafter I can survive, I told myself.

As I see the actor's car leave with my Leema in it, I get that feeling of strength again.

It isn't going to be easy for KK or her parents when they rush home from their Singapore holiday on hearing what has happened. Lives will fall apart. But life will heal itself.

Maybe the drive into the sunset will end with a flat tyre or puppy poo on the floor. Maybe her obsessive cleaning will vex him. Maybe his mood swings will worry her. So many maybes. So much that can go wrong. But until they try it, how will they know?

And so my alphabet book ends. I know the Zigarthanda should start with a J, but this is my alphabet book. What is right for the world may not be right for me. I have always called it Zigarthanda and this shall be my Z.

The drink with a cold heart. The drink that makes you step into the unknown, not thinking about what you have left behind or what lies ahead.

Acknowledgements

Luigi Brioschi, President and Publishing Director, Ugo Guanda Editore, for steering me towards the writing of this book.

Karthika V.K., my editor and publisher in India, as always, for support, advise and camaraderie.

Leela Kalyanaraman for introducing me to the arisi appalam which is where it all began and then demanding I give her a happy ending. For the filter coffee, her colourful Tamizh phrases and for that time in Coonoor which is where the story was born.

Shyam Prasad in Chennai, who listened without once asking why. Such is the true realm of friendship.

My brother Dr P.K. Sunil and sister-in-law Rajini, who opened their home in Valparai to me and gave me the perfect setting I was looking for. Suresh Parambath and Maitreya Nair Parambath for being there, no questions asked. Soumini and Bhaskaran, my parents, who nurtured my taste in food and showed me the wisdom of ingredients.

And Jojo Vasudevan aka Kunchacko, who sat on my lap as I wrote the first page and came back just in time to perch on my lap again as I wrote the last page. One needs a white ball of fur with a tail attached to bring magic into the writing. Thank you, Jayapriya, Harish and Miel for sharing him.